A GOOD WAY TO DIE ...
A GENTLE WAY TO KILL

They staked Luc out. Naked, his limbs were stretched tight by leather thongs that had been soaked in water. As the strips dried and shrank, they cut painfully into his wrists and ankles.

Ascham was watching, making a big deal out of being part of this. But like most real cowards, he made sure he didn't see too clearly. He looked down at the stretched-out figure and said, "Make him tell me what I want to know."

Rosie looked at Luc. The Frenchman closed his eyes once. A sign of assent. Rosie took the pliers from Ascham's goon. He knew what he had to do, but he didn't have to take away Luc's dignity. He'd take his life but leave him that.

COLD
VENGEANCE

Mike McCray

A DELL BOOK

Published by
Dell Publishing Co., Inc.
1 Dag Hammarskjold Plaza
New York, New York 10017

Dell ® TM 681510, Dell Publishing Co., Inc.

ISBN: 0-440-11313-X

Printed in the United States of America

First printing—August 1984

For James Mulkey McDowell, USN

For better are they in a hero's grave
   Than the serfs of time and breath,
For they are the children of the brave,
   And the cherubim of death!

           —James R. Randall,
             "Battle Cry of the South"

1

The boy had been left alone.

The men who called themselves the Black Berets had flown off three weeks ago. The boy was asked to stay and watch the farm, to care for it until they returned. He didn't mind living by himself on the sixty-acre farm a dozen miles outside of Shreveport. That sort of loneliness had been a given in his life. His only break from it had come three months earlier, when he had met Billy Leaps Beeker. Billy Leaps was a Cherokee, just like the boy.

Billy Leaps had saved the boy from torture and death at the hands of two drunken Louisiana rednecks. The boy, wheezing with broken ribs, had watched his rescuer bury the mangled bodies of the two men in the soft dirt floor of the pine forest.

For a short while it had been just the boy and Beeker alone on the farm. Billy Leaps had cared for the boy while he recuperated from the wounds the dead man had inflicted on him. Together they talked the Old Language, but their exchanges were halting. Billy Leaps wasn't fluent in it—he was after all only a half-breed. The boy was a pure Cherokee—but he was mute.

The boy had allowed himself dreams during that time. Billy Leaps brought portions of broth and medicines from the modern doctor and then for hours on end recounted the legends of the Cherokee and the honor of the tribe's warriors. For that—above all—was what the boy had seen in Billy Leaps, that he was a true warrior, just like those in the legends. To hear this man speak of those Cherokee heroes filled the boy with pride. And hope, that he might someday prove himself as well.

The hope hurt more than all the former loneliness. That loneliness had been always with him. He had never acknowledged it, never allowed himself to imagine that life would ever be any

7

other way for him. But now that he had seen the possibility of something better, he was fearful that it could all be snatched away from him. All his pleasure in the companionship of Billy Leaps Beeker, the Cherokee warrior who might lead him into a manly adulthood, was embittered with the fear that some catastrophe would intervene. The welfare authorities, who had shunted him from orphanage to foster home to foster home and back to orphanage again, would suddenly decide that a divorced Cherokee Indian on a remote farm was not a fit guardian for the boy. They'd take him away, and he'd begin another round of foster homes and the orphanage. Or Billy Leaps would decide that the boy was an intrusion on his cherished solitude and, however reluctantly, would send the boy away.

Or that the team that called itself the Black Berets, with the Cherokee as its leader, would not return from its mission.

The boy thought of that team often. He had wondered, at first, how five men so diverse could work as a unit. And at first they hadn't. But then gradually, over the period of their three-month training here on the farm, they had come together as a unit. The same unit that had worked in Vietnam a decade earlier.

Cowboy had been the first to arrive, Billy Leaps's friend who always hid his eyes with dark glasses, and wore shirts like the cowboys on television, bright with color and pearl snap buttons. Cowboy flew a plane that was kept hidden in one of Billy Leaps's barns. Cowboy cared about only two things, it seemed to the boy: flying, and the expensive white powder he called Vitamin C.

Then the other three that Billy Leaps had rerecruited. Rosie Boone, an enormous black man, with a shining white skull piercing his earlobe, who frightened the boy with his strange, mistrustful looks. The big hairy man they called Harry, or the Greek, whose eyes were always filled with sorrow, and whose shoulders, when he sat apart from the others, sank under some invisible weight. Then the last one, the strangest one, the skinny, wiry man no one else seemed to like. They even made him sleep outside, apart from the rest of them. Marty was skinny, smaller than the boy himself, with pale watery eyes behind thick glasses. But in his frenzy, he could be as strong as any of the others, and he had a strange little habit of blowing things up.

The men had gathered here on the farm just as the ancient Cherokee warriors had gathered years ago, to train and prepare for war. And they had given the boy hope. Hope that he might have this place as a home, where he could learn to be a warrior himself, a warrior such as they were.

He had done what he could to make that hope substantial. He had avoided Rosie and his unexpected outbursts of anger. He had grinned at Cowboy's jokes. He had sat silent by the sorrowful Harry, and had arm-wrestled with Marty, who cheated even when he didn't need to. He had cooked for the men, he had tried to anticipate their needs, and, above all, he had accorded their leader, Billy Leaps Beeker, all the respect that a war chief deserved.

The boy thought of all these things as he walked along a disused logging road that wound through the forested portion of Billy Leaps's property. He carried the hunting bow he had found in Beeker's house. He had been desperate to learn the majestic secrets of the rifles the men had practiced with, but they had been preparing for war then and had no time to teach the boy. He knew that, though it rankled him still to be called boy. He was just sixteen, in the awkward ill-defined space between boy and man.

Every day of the Black Berets' absence, the boy got up with the sun. It was late autumn and there was precious little to be done on the few acres of ground that were cultivated. His chores were soon accomplished. He fed the animals, and afterward made certain that supplies of food and grain remained adequate. Because the men weren't around, he sometimes allowed the boy in him to take over for a little while. He teased the pigs, or he ran with the great black Labrador. But he always kept everything in perfect readiness for the men's return. He would have died rather than allow them to find any part of the farm or the hand-hewn cabin not in order. But when his chores were done, he turned to the bow and arrow. Billy Leaps had left hunting rifles in the house, and there was plenty of ammunition, but he had warned the boy to shoot only for food—he didn't want the boy's presence on the property advertised. In his anxiety to follow Billy Leaps's order, he didn't use the gun at all. He learned to hunt with the silent bow and arrow.

In the three weeks of the Black Berets' absence, he had trained himself with it. He strove not only for accuracy, but for ease. He remembered how the team's M-16s had seemed extensions of their bodies. He wanted to work until the bow felt that way. He succeeded at it, not all the time yet, but on occasion. He hoped that if the men saw how well he had taught himself to use the bow and arrow they would allow him to stay and be a part of them. He hoped—though the hope caused him a sharp and intense pain in his heart—that Billy Leaps Beeker would become like a father to him. The father he'd never had. The father who knew and honored the path of the Cherokee warrior. If only the boy proved himself with the bow and arrow, then perhaps Billy Leaps would be convinced.

The boy had made a target range for himself not far from the house. He reached that place now. In his quiver were a dozen arrows. The target, a hundred feet from where he now stood, was merely the upright trunk of a dead tree. He had wrapped it in three cloth rags, one marking the target's head—the height of his own—a second rag the target's heart, and the third its groin. He took an arrow from the quiver, thinking that he might be able to make a new target for Billy Leaps, one of true leather in the old way, not just this improvised sort.

But he didn't mind the newness of the arrows. Even if they were modern and manufactured of aluminum, rather than constructed of wood with chiseled stone heads. The boy knew from the hunting magazines in Beeker's house that these arrows, with their great strength and lightness, would travel far and true from a master archer's bow. The tips were also metal, but sharpened to a degree that would have been impossible to achieve with stone. The boy had nicked his finger once on one of the arrowheads. Without any pressure the blade had cut through nearly half an inch of skin. The blood had gushed. He understood now how such an arrow could pierce the breast of a buck and bring it a swift death.

The boy took aim at his target's head. His arm struggled with the great tension of the bow. It always did the first time. Then he could gauge it for the rest of the session. He sighted carefully and released the arrow. It hit right on the mark, just where the head of a man the boy's size would be. The boy smiled.

10

Then his body froze. So suddenly and completely that even the smile remained graven on his face.

He had heard a strange noise. The boy, who could make no noise himself, was acutely aware of sound. A vehicle was approaching the house. The Black Berets had returned! He turned and made two hurrying steps toward the logging track that would take him back. Then he stopped, just as suddenly as before. Why had they not returned in the plane, as they had left? He was puzzled, and then nervous. And then cautious.

His caution was confirmed a moment later. The Labrador, tethered by a chair to a corner of the house, began to bark. He would not have, had it been Billy Leaps and his men who were returning.

The boy retrieved his arrow from the target and replaced it in his quiver. He crossed stealthily through the forest, approaching the clearing in which Billy Leaps's cabin sat. He was hidden behind underbrush, and waited as the vehicle approached.

It was a Jeep Wagoneer, a common vehicle in this part of the country. The Wagoneer drove up to the cabin fearlessly, as though the driver knew that the Black Berets were absent, as though he had no idea that anyone had been left to guard the place.

The boy watched. Three men got out of the Wagoneer. He recognized none of them. They were laughing and talking. One man's voice was louder than the others'. The boy heard him say, "Tell y'all something, Parkes is gonna be grateful for this one. Even if there's not gonna be much to it. I don't know nothin' about it, but I'll bet my ass Beeker really fucked 'im over."

All three men moved to the back of the four-wheel drive station wagon. The man who had spoken was obviously in charge. He opened the back, and pulled aside a loose tarp. The other two men reached inside and withdrew metal cans, evidently filled with liquid. One went toward the house, the other toward the barn.

The boy knew that the containers held either gasoline or kerosene. They were going to burn the place down.

One man kicked open the door of the cabin, and began sloshing the liquid out of the can even before he was well inside. The

11

other man went inside the barn, and disappeared from the boy's sight.

The boy was terrified. Not for his personal safety, but because he had been left to watch the farm. This was his responsibility!

But then, quite suddenly, his fear was overcome with anger, that these three men should dare to burn the farm owned by Billy Leaps Beeker, the war chief, the leader of the Black Berets, the man the boy hoped . . .

He knew what he had to do.

The one who was leader still stood beside the jeep. He called out toward the man in the house, "James, get it in the corners! A house don't burn right 'less the fire gets in the corners. And the beds, too. Beds is always good."

Then he turned toward the barn and yelled, "Bob, how you doin' in there? You gone need some more? We got plenty!"

"I'm fine!" a voice called back, echoing from inside the barn.

The boy thought for a brief moment.

None of the three had been holding a weapon, though he could see several hunting rifles lying next to the gasoline cans in the rear of the jeep. He couldn't let the men get to those. And that meant he had to get the man closest to the rifles first. That was the leader. And that was just fine.

The boy moved into the clearing. He avoided the fallen branches he could see, and tried not to make any noise whatever. He had an arrow out of the quiver, the one he had retrieved from the target. He swiftly calculated how much taller the leader was than the target, and compensated as well for the greater distance.

This first shot had to be perfect. If he missed they'd be after him with the rifles. And these men were destroyers—they would have no mercy. He had to kill the leader, and not only kill him, but silence him immediately. And he had to hurry. The other two would be soon finished with the cans of flammable liquid.

The boy pulled back the bow, aimed the arrow, and as he released it he prayed a prayer to the gods of the Cherokee.

Four razor-sharp points pierced the leader's neck. The arrow sank deep and clean into his throat. His hands jumped up to grab the arrow, though he had no idea what the sudden, painful, unexpected intrusion was. His mouth opened to scream, but what came out was not sound but a geyser of blood that splashed over the side windows of the jeep, coating them thickly in red.

The blood pulsed out of the hole made in his throat three times, for three beats of his heart. But then he was dead and his heart wasn't beating anymore, and the fountain of red blood became no more than a sullen slow stream. He crumpled to the ground, sliding down the side of the car until he came to rest in an awkward crouch beside the back wheel.

The boy was frightened the other two men would hear the noise, or see the blood on the windows, but the men were busy lighting matches. The fire in the house began with a *whoosh*, but before even that sound had peaked into a bellow, it was matched by another from the other side of the clearing. The barn was starting to go up as well.

The boy, with grim determination on his face, ran behind the jeep. The man who had torched the barn was closer. He would die next. His back was to the boy, his hands on his hips as he stared through the open doors into the brightening interior of the barn. He craned his neck with pleasure to look at the white smoke that had started to seep through the cracks in the roof.

A new arrow was notched in the boy's bow. He aimed at the man's broad back, just where he calculated his heart to be. The arrow was released with a *twang* that sounded musically in the boy's ear. The aluminum shaft, following the four razor-sharp points, sank deep into the man's back. He collapsed onto the earth, within the wavering shadow cast by the burning barn.

Quickly grabbing another arrow from the quiver, the boy raced to the front of the jeep. One intruder remained. The house that Billy Leaps Beeker had built with his own hands was on fire. The boy could see flames through the open doorway and the window to his left. The bed the boy had slept on for the past three months was burning.

The man who had set the fire stood with his back to the house. With an expression of confusion and horror on his face, he was pointing at the body of the group's leader, crouched in the dirt next to the bloodied jeep. The corpse knelt in a coagulating pool of its own blood.

"Bob!" he screamed. "Bob!"

He started to run for the barn, but after a couple of lurching

13

steps, he stopped. He had seen Bob's body, lying in the shadows. He went no closer. He looked all around, his head swiveling rapidly.

The boy rose up slowly from behind the station wagon. He held his bow in one hand, the third arrow in his other.

The boy's appearance triggered something in the third man. He had seen his two friends dead, and now here was a boy. He didn't even immediately make the connection that the boy might be personally responsible for the two deaths. That didn't matter. By just being there, the boy was going to fucking pay. The man took two aggressive steps toward the boy. "You little bas—"

He never finished the word or the thought because there was an arrow in his brain. Four sharpened blades in the shape of an X had sliced through his forehead, his skull, and then through the convolutions of his brain, severing all thought, all sensation, all life in a hundredth of a second. He was, and then, a hundredth second later, he ceased to be.

With a fourth arrow strung in readiness, the boy went to each of the men, to make sure he was dead, and to study the wounds. It wasn't something he wanted to do, but it was a situation that he knew he had to take advantage of. He had never killed a man before. Now he had killed three, not coldly but with malice and vengeance in his heart—and he had to see how good his aim was.

The man he had killed last was certainly dead. The arrow had pierced his brow, at a spot directly between his eyes.

He knelt by the back door of the station wagon and peered into the unseeing eyes of the leader of the three men. The wound in his neck was large and gaping, but the blood had ceased to flow. There was proof of death.

The boy moved into the shadow of the barn. The man lying in the dirt there was still alive. The arrow had pierced his back, and come out through the front. He had fallen on it, and bent the savage head against the earth. But it had evidently missed his heart, though his labored breathing told that very probably a lung had been punctured.

The boy, who had been squatting off a little ways, stood up. Now he felt squeamish, like the man who thinks he's brought down the greatest buck of the forest, only to come closer and find the regal animal in dismal suffering. He was ashamed of his lack of skill, and his squeamishness. There was only one thing to be done. He took the hunting knife out of his belt, where he always carried it, and walked up to the prone body on the ground. He grabbed the man's head by the hair and lifted it up. He gurgled in his throat, and blood spat up out of his mouth onto the ground. The boy brought the edge of his knife to the front of the man's neck and sliced once across, very hard and quickly.

Blood spewed out in a fan shape. Some of the drops flew so high and hard that they splattered against the burning timbers of the barn and sizzled.

The boy let go the corpse's hair. He heard the bones of the corpse's face crack as the head bounced against the hard earth. He looked around. Two of the three buildings that made up the modest compound were in hopeless flames. Only Cowboy's ersatz airplane hangar remained. But the day was bright and there was little smoke. They were far from the road, and that road was little traveled anyway. There was some hope that the fire would not be discovered or reported. The boy ran to the pig pen, much too near the barn, and released the frightened animals. He would be able to gather them later. The Labrador was tethered to the house, and was frantically pulling at the extremity of his chain. The boy let him loose. The fowl inside the barn were already incinerated. He could smell them.

It took nearly all his strength to lift the heavy bodies of the three men into the back of the Wagoneer. He stifled his revulsion at handling the dead for the first time. There was no room for squeamishness now—he had to remove the three arrows from the bodies, no easy task. By the time he was done, and had manipulated the corpses into the jeep, he was drenched with the blood that had flowed out of the open wounds of the first three men that he had ever killed.

He had learned to drive Billy Leaps's pickup, so the automatic station wagon proved no difficulty for him. He stripped off his blood-soaked clothes, climbed into the front seat, and slowly drove the car off Billy Leaps's property. Despite the chill of the day, he kept the windows of the automobile down. The stink of blood and death was still nearly overpowering. He drove the Wagoneer down a side road onto property owned by a paper mill in Shreveport. A mile into the forest, he turned off the logging track and simply drove as far and as deep into the forest as he could go. When the jeep stuck in a ravine, the boy wiped the steering wheel clean of his fingerprints—though he knew many others must still rest on other parts of the car, and on the corpses themselves—and climbed out through the window. Barefoot, wrapped in a dirty blanket he had found in the back seat, the boy walked back to the farm.

The house and the barn that had been given over to his protection were smoldering mounds of charred and blackened timbers. They stank of gasoline and incinerated chickens. The boy went around slowly in the clearing, obliterating the tracks of the station wagon, and then kicked dirt into the three pools of blood in the desolate yard.

In the barnlike hangar he made himself a bed of straw, and placing his bow and his arrows beside it, he covered his shivering limbs with the blanket and once more took up his wait for the return of the Black Berets.

2

Billy Leaps Beeker sat in a hotel room in San Francisco. As he looked about, he realized that *room* was not an adequate term for what Marty had insisted on renting for the team. They were housed in a suite of six interconnecting rooms, three baths, with more beds and windows than any of them had patience to count, and greater views than anybody could stare at for more than half an hour at a time. Marty had insisted on it, though the suite was costing more than a thousand dollars a day. But there was no reason not to spend the money. Marty had it.

They all had it.

The Black Berets had gotten very rich very quickly.

Parkes, an ex-CIA man they had known and mistrusted in Vietnam, had called them together again, hinted that he was still connected with the Company—the CIA—and sent them on a mission to Laos, ostensibly to rescue eighteen Americans still being held prisoner, though the war had been over for many years.

On this clandestine, unlawful mission the team went in, was attacked, fought back, and overcame their Laotian adversaries. But they didn't find the eighteen Americans who were being held prisoner. They found burned poppy fields, and discovered that Parkes's real business in Laos was opium. The men the Black Berets had slaughtered were merely rebellious underlings. Parkes, the ex-CIA man, was no more than a glorified drug pusher. Billy Leaps had figured this out just in time to keep from getting himself and his team killed as well. When they came away, they brought out the fortune that had been secreted in the Laotian stronghold. It was inadequate recompense for the treachery.

The fortune was in gold and precious stones. They had con-

17

verted it to cash and securities in Bangkok, and had flown back to the United States as very rich, very bitter men.

Beeker sat in a chair that was turned toward the magnificent view of the Golden Gate Bridge in the late afternoon sunlight. He pondered the number of questions that desperately wanted answering in his mind. Had Parkes operated wholly on his own? Or did he really have the backing of the CIA? Was Parkes an outlaw even to his agency? Who knew of their mission? Or of their success?

Beeker did not think they could have returned to this country unobserved. They were hardly the bunch to fade into the background at airports, or at customs. Marty was making no secret of the new-gotten wealth. Beeker knew that sooner or later Parkes would come after them.

And that was just fine with Beeker.

Parkes had something coming to him. And he was going to be very, very sorry to get it.

Beeker turned around in his chair at sudden laughter behind him.

Cowboy and Rosie were sitting on chairs, facing one another, leaning forward, and passing a joint back and forth. They were both high on the dynamite weed that the black man had scored in the Fillmore district. Beeker had forbidden the men any drugs while they were in the field. But they were back now, in civilization. And civilization, Beeker snorted to himself, meant drugs and alcohol, women and parties, hotel suites and big shiny cars. *Civilization!*

Marty and the Greek had gone off somewhere earlier. The Greek was the only one who really actually liked Marty, the only one who would put up with the man who was such a volatile mixture of gangly adolescent and frenzied psychopath. They'd be in a bar, and Marty would be loudly recounting their adventures in Laos, as if Harry were a perfect stranger. And Marty would be doing it to impress the bartender, to impress the woman sitting in the booth behind him, or the guys at the next table.

Beeker just wanted out of San Francisco. The luxury of this hotel suite meant nothing to him. He wanted only to get back to the farm, and the boy who he knew would be waiting for him.

18

He wished he could call the kid, but the kid was mute, and would not answer the telephone.

It was strange that he worried so much about the boy. Obviously it had a lot to do with their both being Cherokee. And with Beeker not being married anymore. Beeker knew he'd never marry again, and therefore he'd never have a son. He'd resigned himself to that, at least until this kid came along. Beeker saw in the boy the kind of son he would have chosen over all others, if fathers ever got that sort of choice. A youngster who had obvious pride and ability, who continually proved himself trustworthy and even courageous.

The afternoon light became golden, and the Golden Gate Bridge resplendent with the reflection. Billy Leaps's mind alternated between the two thoughts: the boy back on the farm, and revenge against Parkes, who had betrayed them.

Cowboy Hatcher was watching Billy Leaps stare out the window. Rosie Boone's stoned monologue flowed in and out of his mind. Some of it registered, but most of it didn't. Cowboy was thinking about something else. He was imagining Beeker's thoughts at that moment.

It didn't matter to Beeker how much bullion and gems they had taken out of the jungle. He didn't care how rich they were now, how many beds they could sleep on, how many women they could screw, how many fancy restaurants they could walk into without worrying about the prices on the menu. None of that made any difference to Beeker, because Beeker felt that he had betrayed his men.

Betrayed them because he had misrepresented the mission to them.

They hadn't gone into Laos to rescue eighteen MIAs rotting in pits dug in the earth. They had gone into Laos to protect Parkes's opium investment.

Beeker felt bad, Cowboy was sure, because he had gathered the men together again for a purpose that at base was cowardly and ignoble.

It didn't matter to Beeker that none of his men felt betrayed.

None of them, Cowboy was convinced, had really believed in the reality of those eighteen POWs. They hadn't cared about that because they were back together again. The team that had been the most fearsome, the most awesomely competent squad in the entire mangled history of the Vietnam War had been regrouped by Beeker.

So who cared what the mission was?

All the men knew, all they cared about, was that they were together again. After years of being wasted. Years of going to pot. Harry the Greek, Haralambos Georgeos Pappathanassiou, had ended up tending bar in Chicago after the war. Harry, who had known so much, learned so much, experienced so much in the war as the gutsiest, hardest fighting man the Navy SEALs had ever produced, had ended up with a rag in hand, wiping up beer along the surface of a fifteen-foot mahogany bar for a dozen hours a day. Harry had lost his soul in Vietnam, but that had happened to a lot of men. That bar in Chicago had taken away his self-respect and his manhood.

Or Rosie, feared, awesome Roosevelt Boone, the man who had taught himself to kill and torture the way other men learned to tune a Chevy motor or fill out a tax form. If Rosie's orders were to maim, he maimed; and if to slaughter, then he slaughtered. How had he ended up? He made bandages for burn victims. Made bandages by peeling the skin off corpses in the subbasement of a municipal hospital in Newark, New Jersey. It wasn't a job for just anybody, but then a well-trained killer didn't have many employment options in a peacetime nation.

Applebaum? Crazy, crazy Marty Applebaum. Marty liked to blow things up. He boasted that he once blew up a swimming pool, though nobody had ever figured out how that was possible, since it was already just a hole in the ground. But if anybody could do it, Marty could. Marty had to prove himself every minute of the day—and in combat he could show that he really was fearless. And what had they sent Applebaum back to? The painstaking demolition of rotted factories, play time with old bricks, half a dozen carefully placed sticks of damp dynamite instead of the most powerful arsenal in the world.

And what about himself? Cowboy thought. Flying dope runs to Latin America. A two-bit smuggler who one day just might get caught. And he was the man who used to fly with God. The man who could have taken a canoe, stuck on a set of ceiling-fan blades, twisted a rubber-band motor, and rescued half a dozen wounded men under artillery fire during a monsoon. Well, maybe that was a slight exaggeration, but it wasn't much of one.

They had all lost themselves when they came back Stateside. There were no parades for these heroes. They were the despised symbols of a war that had been lost, not by them, but by the fucking politicians and the fucking undercutting CIA. Why had they ever gone to Vietnam if they weren't intended to win? Why did they have to come home and have their women and children glance away from them in shame because of what they had done under orders?

But Beeker, Cowboy thought as he turned back to the leader, Beeker never wavered, no matter what they threw at him. His were the values that were consistent, honorable, steadfast. Billy Leaps had been that way during the war, and he continued that way now. So when the call had come to regroup, to form the team again, they had jumped on the opportunity as heaven-sent. Not heaven-sent. Hell-sent. They had been made devils in Vietnam. And devils just weren't happy in a peacetime paradise. So when Beeker had recalled them to hell, there wasn't one who hesitated to fling himself down into the pit.

So it didn't matter to the members of the Black Berets team that the mission had been a false one. They would have died fighting it, and died gladly. Because they were men, fighting under a man they perceived as better than themselves. They were soldiers, and they respected their leader and cared nothing for whatever leader might be over him. Once they had learned these truths they knew it would be impossible for them to move back into the complacency of American life and its make-believe games of career and suburbia and community respectability.

There are men in this world, Cowboy thought, who are born to be soldiers. Billy Leaps Beeker was one. Then there are men in this world who become soldiers, who face death and oblivion and come out, not the walking wounded of the psych wards, not the shaken ones who wake up screaming at night and wish like the damned wish that it had never happened to them, but the ones who walk out the other side of battle. Hardened. Calloused. Scarred. But ready for the next one.

"That's us," said Cowboy aloud.

"What?" Rosie asked. Rosie had been talking about how much more dope cost now than it had back in '72.

"We're the ones who became soldiers," said Cowboy. Then he pointed at the back of Billy Leaps's chair. "He was born one."

"Cowboy," said Rosie, "you are *stoned*. You need a drink." He got up and went over to the fully-equipped bar that came with the suite. Rosie was pouring a glass of good scotch when the phone rang. He picked up the receiver.

"Beeker, it's for you."

The leader stood. His six-one bulk, a medical textbook illustration of hardened muscle that was apparent under any type of clothing, strode across the room. Beeker took the speaker from the big black man's hand.

The call could be only bad news. Only their enemies had any interest in them. There were no friends to call the members of the Black Berets.

Beeker steeled himself for Parkes's voice. Wheedling Parkes, who'd try to make Beeker believe that he and his men hadn't been betrayed after all, that it was all just a great big misunderstanding, and wasn't it time now to turn over the fortune they had managed to smuggle out of Laos?

But it wasn't Parkes on the telephone.

The voice was female. And not only female, it was feminine and soft.

"Welcome home, soldier."

"Marine," Beeker contradicted her.

"Marine. I'm in Suite 1534. Directly below you. I heard you walk across the room to pick up the phone. Will you come see me?"

Beeker hung up without replying. Then he spoke to Cowboy and Rosie. "I'll be back," he said.

Neither man asked where Beeker was going. No one ever asked Billy Leaps Beeker where he was going or what he intended to do once he got there.

3

He stood in front of the door to the fifteenth-floor suite and wondered if this was a setup. An ambush. But all his instincts told him no. He trusted those instincts—they had kept him alive at least this long. He knocked.

Delilah answered the door almost immediately. Her smile was outlined with that kind of lipstick that always looked wet. Her skin was creamy, milky-white, and soft as the only time he had seen her before. Beeker experienced an involuntary contraction of his chest and his breath, the kind of twinge he wasn't used to.

She stood aside and waved him in. "I'm surprised you didn't come in with guns blazing," she said lightly.

"Is that what I should have done?" Beeker asked. He had moved in only far enough to let the door close behind him.

She walked away from him into a room identical to the one that was directly above. Only the drapes were of a different pattern. Her strong, pleasant perfume wafted through the air in her wake. He liked it. Usually he reacted against strong scents on women, but he liked this one. He felt the twinge again, and this time it wasn't in his chest. It was farther down.

"I know you don't drink a whole lot," she said with the trace of a southern accent, "but at least a glass of wine?"

He shrugged. He watched her pour two goblets and take one of them over to a chair by the window. She sat down, wrapping her legs up underneath herself. She was studying him. Another man might have taken her attention as a compliment, or a come-on. Beeker knew it was an evaluation. He wasn't at all certain it had anything to do with the twinge he felt when he studied her.

She wouldn't speak, it appeared, until he had joined her. He took up the goblet of wine from the table, and seated himself in

23

the chair facing hers. His stance was as stiff and military as hers was relaxed and seductive. His legs were wide apart, his forearms resting on his knees. He held the glass in both hands and stared down into the red depths of the wine.

"When we found out that Gouglemann wasn't really there, it was too late to stop you," she finally said.

Beeker simply nodded his head. Gouglemann, an old Vietnam comrade, had been dead for a dozen years. Parkes had said he was alive and being held captive in Laos. Gouglemann was the reason the Black Berets had gone in. Beeker had expected to hear this excuse somewhere along the line. It's what Parkes himself would have said. So Beeker said nothing in return. He wanted to hear what this woman had to say. He didn't even want to look at her. He could judge her truthfulness by her voice, but only if he weren't distracted. And if he looked at her, one thing was certain—he wouldn't be conducting a lie detector test.

"It was too late to stop you," she repeated, "but we tried anyway."

"How?" asked Beeker, still staring down into the wine. "Did you leave a message at the hotel? And then found out we'd already left for the jungle?"

"No," she said. "We blew up the ammunition dump."

He looked up once, quickly, then back down again. That surprised him.

"You thought that was a Parkes double-cross, didn't you? It wasn't. Our men did that. They thought it would turn you back. You can't carry out a mission without proper supplies, and you had made it very clear what you needed. So if that dump was destroyed, then the Black Berets would give up their plan. I told them it wouldn't work. I was right. So now my people have decided that you are either extraordinarily brave, or just plain crazy."

"Your organization, your people—you keep talking about them. When I met you in Las Vegas you told me you weren't with Parkes."

"No."

"Are you Agency?"

She laughed, and Beeker looked up quickly. The laughter was soft, but somewhere behind it was real strength. "No, I'm not

24

Agency. Where's my three-piece suit with a rep tie? My trench coat and wing tips? You know, there are women in the CIA. But if you met one, you'd swear that's what she was wearing."

Beeker looked at her once again. Delilah wasn't dressed in any manner to conform to that image. She wore one of those dresses he had never really understood. It might have been appropriate for a formal dinner in a secluded corner of a discreet and expensive restaurant, or it might have been the nightgown a woman wore when she was bent on seducing a particular man on a particular occasion.

That same creamy white skin showed at the tops of her breasts. In the deep cleft of her gown, the mounds of flesh seemed large, soft, and inviting. Beeker kept both hands on his glass because he was afraid that if he didn't, he'd reach out and touch them. Stroke the tops. Push down the soft clinging material and brush the nipples he could already see in outline. Cup underneath the breasts and weigh them. The twinge had grown into a steady pulse.

He cleared his throat. "If you're not Agency, and not Parkes, who are you?"

She averted her eyes for one moment. "I honestly can't tell you. Not now at any rate."

"What's Prometheus?"

She sighed, as if with relief that he did not press her on the question of her allegiances. "Prometheus is Parkes's own game. He set it up with two other men out of the Agency. No legal standing. It's not part of policy."

"But does the Agency approve of Parkes?"

"When something Parkes does helps them, yes, they do approve. When something Parkes does is incredibly stupid and goes completely against American interests, then no they don't approve. But they don't have to take the blame either. That's pretty simple, admittedly, but that's how they think in Langley." She mentioned the CIA headquarters with something that was between distaste and contempt. She put her goblet of wine aside. Her tone now lost just a little of its former feminine softness. Beeker actually liked that. She was warming to her subject—it seemed to fascinate her. "Let me try to explain to you how this situation came about. I'm talking about Prometheus, and the

25

other organizations like it. During Carter's administration, a lo⁺ of restrictions were placed on covert activity. The Agency was under almost continual scrutiny. Its files were opened for all and sundry to look at and complain about. The Agency thought it was going to lose all its power. So it spun off. It tossed out a couple of dozen of its middle-level agents and operatives—the ones with the biggest entrepreneurial spirits—and said, in effect, 'Go to it.' Parkes was one of them, and Parkes set up Prometheus.''

"But there are others?'' Beeker asked. He felt he could look at her now, for they were, in a real sense, talking business.

"About a dozen were set up originally, but a few were disbanded, others petered out. There are about five left, I think. Prometheus is one, but it's certainly not the biggest. Or the most reliable, I might add. Sometimes they're given funds, and sometimes they manage on their own. The only thing the Agency always provides is information—simple because it's practically impossible to monitor that. The CIA, if it wanted to, could beam the entire files of the IRS into a trapper's hut in Siberia, and nobody would ever know about it except the trapper.''

She paused for a few moments. Beeker nodded with a slight smile. She was telling him everything she could. She worked for another of those secret subagencies. Her organization wasn't entirely in CIA control, but they were—you might say—in the CIA Commonwealth.

"Some of these spin-off organizations have become outlaws,'' Delilah went on. "There's no other word for them. They're after money and power. Others have kept their ideals, and when it's necessary they step outside the law. But they do that, ultimately, in order to *protect* the law for everybody else.''

"I heard this part before,'' said Beeker. "It doesn't work.''

Delilah was suddenly earnest. "It *does* work. I've *seen* it work. It *has* to work. Because the future of this whole country—and the values this country represents—may just depend on how well we do our work. We have the secrecy that the CIA used to have. There are four or five organizations operating in this country that could raise an army to equal, say, Canada's. We could raise it in five days, and you'd never hear a word about it.'' She said this with pride.

"It sounds like Vietnam,'' Beeker commented. "A real mess.

Twenty-five groups running around, every one of them with a little power. Every one of them with a different goal. Every one of them made up of a whole goddamn set of greedy bastards. Every one of them working for a different purpose. You're glad I screwed Parkes up because Parkes is on a different team, that's all.''

Delilah shook her head. "That's not it at all," she said. "Parkes was getting dangerous. He wasn't reliable.''

"This sounds like infighting," said Beeker, waving a hand in disgust. "I trained as a Marine, and that's all. I had my place in the war, and I stood in it. I had my duty in the war, and I performed it. I don't know shit about policy. I have to have two things to operate efficiently. I have to have my rifle, and I have to have trust in whoever is giving me orders. I've still got my M-16. But when I put trust in Parkes, I got screwed. And the fact is, I don't trust you either.''

"I'm not trying to give you orders.''

"No?''

"I'm trying to make it easier for you to get what you want.'' There was more than a hint of seductiveness in this.

"What is it I want?''

"You want Parkes," said Delilah. She said that as if she had said *You want my body*. And that was all right, except that Beeker probably wanted Parkes more.

"I want him bad," Beeker admitted.

"So do we.''

"Why?''

"We've figured out some things about the mission he sent you on," said Delilah. "We don't like them." She went to the sideboard and refilled her glass. As she went on, she brought the bottle over and poured more for Beeker as well. Her actions were automatic, for she was thinking only of Parkes and the shadowy organizations that operated outside anyone's control, but she remained graceful, seductive. "Parkes hadn't been cut out of that heroin trade. He was still getting his share. What he wanted was that fortune that you brought out with you.''

Beeker said nothing.

"Yes," she said, "we know about the gold and the jewels. In

fact, I've seen some of the emeralds you sold in Bangkok. They were gorgeous. I even bought one—a little one—for myself.''

Beeker said nothing. Everything had been sold in Bangkok, converted into cash. He looked at her closely and asked, with a note of sarcasm, ''Are you letting us keep the money we risked our lives for?''

''We're going to let you consider it as payment,'' said Delilah.

''For what?''

''For getting Parkes.'' She smiled, and her smile was warm. It was as if, with that directive, all the business of the evening had been set aside. That smile brought back the twinge to Beeker's chest. It was echoed and amplified in his loins. It became the regular throb. He sat still and watched as her body quickly relaxed, as though in immediate response to a command her brain had sent straight down her torso.

Even her dress seemed to have changed. It certainly no longer could have been worn to a restaurant. Now it was almost certainly a gown meant solely for the bedroom—the kind of nightgown a woman wore to make a man want her, and want her bad.

She didn't really run her hands over her breasts, but the movement she made was as openly sensual as that; Billy Leaps responded emphatically.

Delilah moved over to him. She was able to make gestures that would have seemed vulgar on almost any other woman. She took his wine glass from his hand and put it on a nearby table. She slid up onto his knee. She put one soft hand behind his neck.

Beeker had had many women. Women of all sorts and descriptions. He had even loved some of them for a while. He had obviously known aggressive women. But none to compare to Delilah as she was now.

He expected her to kiss him. Instead she unbuttoned his shirt, starting at the top. Her long fingernails chipping at his chest beneath as she stared into his eyes and smiled. Still without removing her gaze from his, she pulled his undershirt up out of the constraint of his belted slacks.

He looked only into her eyes. He felt her hands caress his stomach. Again, when she moved forward, he expected her to kiss him. Instead, her mouth went to the scarred tissue of his right ear. A bullet in Vietnam had taken away half that flesh, leaving a physical indication of what had happened in Billy Leaps's soul as well.

Most often women shrank from that piece of mangled flesh, feeling fear and even disgust for the disfigurement. A few women were fascinated by it, and he'd find them staring at it. One or two had even touched it, and run a finger along its ragged seams. But he couldn't remember one woman who had ever put it into her mouth.

Other women wanted him *despite* his torn ear. Delilah alone recognized that it was part of him, that it was a picture of his wounded soul, that—paradoxically—Billy Leaps Beeker wouldn't have been whole if the ear had been intact.

He felt her tongue run over the rough flesh. Her breath was hot. In such close proximity her breasts pressed hard against his body, their fullness a sexual delight and her warmth beneath the gown providing even greater fuel for the hot pulse that was beginning to overpower him.

He knew that it would be easy to take her. But this was interesting. He wanted to see what would happen if he let her lead the way. Just what did she have in mind? In a very few minutes, after they had moved into the bedroom, he found out.

Delilah stood at the foot of the bed, her tongue moving along her lips, making them appear wetter than before. He was naked now, erect but making no other move, determined to show that not even her obvious availability and voluptuousness were going to overpower his self-control.

"If you want it," he said, "you have to come for it."

Delilah lost the showdown. She wore only her gown, nothing else. It came off, too quickly. She climbed onto the bed and straddled Billy Leaps. His grin was one of triumph, but he hadn't won yet. Her moist warmth fired his midsection. He couldn't keep his hips from lifting her up. The desire, and the fulfilling of that desire, were automatic.

She smiled as though she knew what Beeker had said with just that single thrust. She smiled as though they were even now.

She collapsed on top of him and brought their mouths together. She helped him enter her.

4

The boy heard the plane's engines long before he saw the twin-propellered Beechcraft approach for its landing. Cowboy's elegant maneuvers brought it down to the ground in a long, liquid movement, one that had no rough edges to it. Cowboy's landings never did.

The boy stood at the open doors of the hangar. He watched as the plane taxied up the slight incline of the narrow asphalt road that was a landing strip in disguise. Its metal wings lifted and fell gently as it came. The boy wore only a few rags he had tied together as a kind of loincloth. His own clothing had been burned in the fire, all but the one set of garments he had been wearing when the arsonists had come to Billy Leaps Beeker's house. But those were heavy and stiff with the dead men's blood, and the boy had buried them.

As soon as the plane stopped, a few dozen feet shy of the hangar, Beeker jumped out of the co-pilot's seat and ran to the boy. He grabbed hold of his head between his two massive fists with such power that the boy was convinced his worst fear had been realized. Beeker was going to blame him for what had happened. It had been his responsibility to protect the farm while the Black Berets were absent and he had failed in it. He waited for one of those huge hands to be drawn back, and to strike him. He did not brace for the pain, knowing he deserved it. He only wondered how many times Beeker would strike. It didn't matter, so long as the punishment ended there. He didn't care how many times Billy Leaps hit him—he didn't care if all five men took their turns—so long as, in the end, they didn't send him away from this place he had dared to think of as home.

Billy Leaps didn't strike, however. And anger wasn't the

30

emotion that infused his face. His steely blue eyes—set so far apart—were frozen on the boy's own. That was not anger. That was the most terrifying, the most awesome sense of relief Billy Leaps Beeker had ever experienced. When he had seen the destruction of his house and barn from the air, Beeker had known that Parkes had come, had sent his goons to attack him in his most vulnerable point. Or what Parkes thought was Billy Leaps's most vulnerable point.

His home.

The house and farm that Beeker had built with his own hands was obviously the single most important thing in his life. That Parkes knew about, that is. How do you rape a warrior? You violate his unguarded home. You burn his house, you scatter his grain to the wind, you broadcast salt in his plowed fields. You put his children to the sword.

That's what Beeker had feared, in the sky, as he stared down from the plane at the destruction below. That Parkes had also found out about the boy.

The boy was alive, and Beeker's heart still burned hot.

Submissively, the boy stared at the ground, still awaiting his punishment. Beeker lifted the boy's head, looked into his eyes, and vowed simply, "You will never be left defenseless again."

Rosie, Applebaum, and Harry the Greek were out of the plane on the ground with most of their luggage. Cowboy rolled the plane into the hangar. As this was the only shelter left standing on the property, the men went inside, and made themselves a place to sit in the corner.

Cowboy had hugged the boy, picked him up off the ground and squeezed him. So had Harry. Rosie put one arm around the boy's shoulder and lifted him up that way, but let go suddenly—it was an awkward movement. Applebaum looked embarrassed and blushed, and shook hands. But they all vibrated with the happiness that the boy still lived. Not one of them, up there in the air, had dared hope it. Not one of them, up there in the air, had dared say to Beeker, "The kid'll be all right. He can take care of himself." It never mattered if a man could take care of himself or not. Sometimes he just got offed, and that was that. Too many of their buddies in Vietnam had died, when everybody had expected and hoped they would come through it alive. But here was the kid, even skinnier than before, nearly naked and shivering with cold—but he was alive.

Cowboy got a blanket from the plane and wrapped the boy in it. They sat down on the straw-strewn floor of the barn, beneath the shadow of one of the wings of the Beechcraft, and the boy told his story. Beeker spoke the words that the boy communicated to him through his own sign language.

The boy's report was thorough. He confirmed what they expected, that Parkes was behind it. The boy had heard the arsonists use his name.

"Fuckin' bastard," Applebaum sneered.

"It's gonna be good to get him," Rosie mused. "Real good."

The boy continued. Beeker translated slowly, for the boy was careful in his telling, making certain that he got everything right. The men couldn't understand why Beeker suddenly raised a hand for the boy to stop. They watched, puzzled, while their leader's darkly tanned face seemed to pale. Something happened behind Beeker's eyes. The expression was a familiar one, though Cowboy had never before seen it in the Cherokee's face. But if not there, where?

On Harry. Billy Leaps's eyes suddenly bore that expression of unbearable sadness, of unrelenting hurt that Cowboy had seen only in the Greek. But there it was.

The men waited silently, curious and expectant, but not daring to press. Finally Beeker spoke. "He killed them. All three of them. With his bow and arrow. And his knife."

The men looked at the youth, shivering though he was wrapped in the striped blanket from the plane. They remembered similar boyish faces from Vietnam, faces much too young to bear such knowledge and experience behind the eyes. Before they went away, he had seemed a child—his emaciated body had helped that illusion. Now that they had returned, he seemed a man—and his wiry frame reminded them a little of Applebaum's. So much potential strength hidden in tendon and slender bone.

Beeker stood up. "The boy had the truck out back, so it wasn't damaged. I'm going into town and get the boy some clothes. Marty, get out a set of gear he can wear till we get him his own. You're small enough your stuff might fit."

"Better than mine," said Rosie, who had enough meat to make up three of the boy.

"Got it, Beeker." Applebaum was infamous for never letting anyone borrow anything of his personal possessions. He was superstitious about what he put next to his skin. But he certainly wasn't going to argue with Billy Leaps about a pair of pants and a shirt at this moment.

He got fatigue trousers and a couple of shirts out of his bag. The boy shyly turned his back to unwrap the loincloth and put on the borrowed garments.

"What are we gonna do?" Rosie asked.

"About what?" Beeker responded. So much had to be done that Beeker, for the moment, couldn't think beyond the necessity of finding clothing for the kid.

"We gotta sleep. We gotta eat. There's nothing left here except straw. What are we gonna do?" the black man repeated.

Billy Leaps went to the door of the hangar, and gazed out at the black, ashen heaps of jutting timbers and refuse that were all that remained of his hand-hewn house and barn. Now that he knew the boy was alive, he could nurse the anger he felt toward Parkes for this attack.

"We're staying here," Beeker decreed. "We've got sleeping bags with our gear, and field stoves too. We'll sleep here in the hangar."

Cowboy started to protest, "Listen, we can *buy* us a hotel—"

"If the boy can live out here, without a roll, without a blanket, without clothes, and without any food—I think the five of us can manage for a few days with all the stuff we have in the plane. But maybe you got soft in San Francisco, Cowboy."

Cowboy scuffed his boots against the barn floor in frustration.

"And tomorrow," Beeker went on, "we start rebuilding."

Rosie and Cowboy groaned in unison. Harry sighed. Applebaum said, "Oh shit . . ."

"This is my land. I will have my house on my own land," said Beeker. He walked off toward the wooded part of his property, where the boy had told him the truck was waiting. A few minutes later, he drove up to the hangar doors. The boy, dressed in Applebaum's camouflage outfit, climbed into the passenger seat. Beeker drove the truck away.

33

"Might as well unload the plane," sighed Cowboy. "We're not gonna change his mind about anything today. Believe me. He's gonna play building house and he's gonna make us play it too. When Beeker says something in that tone of voice, man, it might as well be chiseled in stone."

That night they barbecued three chickens over a charcoal fire. For a place that had just been torched, for a place a group of trained mercenaries called home, for a place where a sixteen-year-old boy had just killed three adults, the farm held a strange sense of peace.

The men ate slowly, enjoying the chicken and talking softly about those things men talk about—women, money, war. They were already at that point again where they spoke aloud in half sentences, or disconnected phrases, while their minds, on a communal wavelength, filled in all the blanks. A stranger might have had considerable difficulty following just what was being said. They seemed to pay almost no attention to the youngster who sat with them in his new clothes, just jeans and a flannel shirt, a pair of construction boots. Cowboy had made one comment: "Gotta get you a hat." It wasn't an offer, it wasn't a suggestion, it was a simple statement of fact. "Man's gotta have a hat."

While the boy liked hearing that—he relished any acknowledgment that the interdependence of the men included him—what Billy Leaps said had an even stronger impact. What Billy Leaps said would totally change the way the boy thought about himself.

He spoke to the adult men, not to the boy. "Cherokee kids usually get Anglo names. This kid's been called 'John' all his life."

"Don't fit," said Rosie.

"No," Beeker agreed. "A full-blooded Cherokee like him is rare, he shouldn't have to carry around a foreign name."

"Yeah," laughed Applebaum, "be like me being called 'Kunte Kinte,' right, Rosie?"

"Right," said Rosie. "When the obvious name for you, Applebaum, would be Asshole Q. Fuckup."

"There's a legend," said Beeker, with a warning glance, "except that it's not a legend, it's fact, about a Cherokee warrior. When the soldiers came into the Southeast, they forced the

34

Cherokee to move to Oklahoma. Except some of them wouldn't go. They ran into the mountains where the soldiers could never get at them.

"This particular warrior I'm talking about became their chief. He was the most famous and respected Indian in the country. The Army gave up trying to fight him. There was no way they could get him out of the mountains. But there weren't enough Indians left east of the Mississippi to give 'em much trouble anyway, so they were willing to compromise with these Cherokee.

"Said the Cherokee could stay and become good citizens of North Carolina. But, there was a murder warrant out for their chief. The government claimed he had killed some white women in a raid. They didn't admit they were fighting a war, but said this warrior was an outlaw, a renegade.

"So they made a deal. The Cherokee could stay in their ancestral home and live happily ever after, but their chief had to give himself up to be hanged. It was a devil's pact, to make their chief—the symbol of their independence—surrender in return for his people's peace. But this chief was a great warrior. He had risked his life a hundred times for the safety of his people. That's what a warrior does. That's what we've done.

"So he just rode into town one day. And the government hanged him. But the government also kept their word. Those Cherokee are still there in the North Carolina mountains. They never even saw Oklahoma."

Beeker paused, remembering his own youth on the godforsaken land that had been the Cherokee's banishment.

"That chief is almost like a mythic god to the Cherokee now. He has the most honored name in the Cherokee world. Our last truly great warrior."

Beeker still did not look at the boy, but he said, "This kid's got a right to a name better than John. He's going to have that warrior's name." At last he did turn to the boy, whose rapt face glowed red from both pride and the coals of the charcoal fire.

"I name you Tsali," said Beeker, "after the great warrior of the Cherokee. You've earned that name."

The boy slowly raised his head. He used sign language to spell out the name. *Tsali*.

35

"Yes," said Billy Leaps Beeker, and then went back to his chicken.

Tsali. The name made the youth's skin crawl with freezing excitement. He blushed with a fierce pride. The stripping away of the Anglo name was powerful enough, but to be given this name in its place was beyond anything he had dreamed.

"Good name, kid," Rosie said. Rosie, that big black man who suddenly didn't seem so frightening to Tsali as he had before. "Good name for you."

"Weird if you ask me," Applebaum grunted.

"Nobody did," said Cowboy quickly. And then wondered just what kind of hat he'd buy for Tsali when he went to town tomorrow.

5

The men were used to the way that Billy Leaps went whole hog at everything he set out to do. He was bound and determined to have his house rebuilt, and if that were so, then there was no reason not to begin the following morning. Early the following morning. Tsali had begun the coffee on a camp stove he must have lighted even before dawn. Beeker was already dressed, walking about the property, figuring out what would go where.

The men were only half awake when he came back to the hangar and sat down with them. Tsali brought the bitter coffee over and poured it into the metal cups they'd retrieved from their packs. There was a chill to the morning air. Even in Louisiana, December brings cold. Applebaum and Cowboy wrapped themselves in their sleeping bags, heaving the heavy down-filled cloth over their shoulders. They still shivered.

"Beeker, we gotta get some more clothes," Cowboy complained. "Sweaters, coats, all that shit."

"And I am *not* eating C rations one more time, not while we're here, anyway," Rosie shouted. "This is goddamn Louisiana, this is not goddamn Laos, and in goddamn Louisiana they got these places where you can buy goddamn hot food." He stared down at the cold food that had been hated by generations of American fighting men. Every time you ate C rations, you hoped it would be the last time. They always came around again.

Beeker waved away their objections. "All in good time."

"Good time, hell," Rosie snarled. "Good time is today, this morning, food, clothes. We're fucking rich bastards, and we're freezing here in summer fatigues and shoveling C rations. This shit's gotta stop."

"Okay," said Beeker easily. He had already planned to give

37

in on this. "We'll draw up a list, and I'll make assignments. We'll all shop in Shreveport this morning. That's okay, 'cause I got to see a contractor, a mason, a plumber, and get them started going.''

"Your new house?" Harry asked.

"Not just that." Beeker smiled. "Our base of operations. This farm is gonna be turned into the most advanced piece of military real estate you ever saw. It's gonna make a Minuteman silo look like a lean-to on the side of an outhouse. We got enough money to do whatever we want. And if you guys don't want in, I've got enough in my share to pull it off solo. I'm not gonna force anybody to spend their money. I'm not gonna force anybody to live down here with me.''

"What are you up to, Beeker?" Cowboy asked. His look was sly.

"It was your idea in the first place, Cowboy. When you built this hangar to look like a barn. And that landing strip to look like a farm road. But I'm not going to be hiding from the narcs, I'm gonna build me a fortress out here. Except nobody's gonna know that's what it is. I'm gonna make sure that I'm ready next time Parkes—or somebody like Parkes—tries to come after me. Or Tsali. Or us.''

"Motherfucking Indian's on the warpath," grumbled Rosie. "I want to buy me a beach, man. I want to buy me a whole goddamn apartment building on the corner where the whores hang out so I can look out of my window all night long, and whistle for 'em to come up, one by one, and two by two. I don't want no fucking Fort Knox in the goddamn Louisiana wilderness. Why not a beach, why not a fucking beach, man? And fish for marlin off a goddamn deck?''

"Because that's not the way men live," said Beeker simply. "And we're gonna live like men.''

Nobody said anything for a few minutes.

"I'm in," said Cowboy after a while. "I'm crazy in the head, but I'm in.''

"Can I get what I want?" asked Applebaum, after clearing his throat. He was just talking about explosives, and everybody knew it.

"You'll get your own dump," said Beeker. "And I'm gonna let you design it."

"I'm in," said Applebaum, with an anticipatory grin. "Harry, you're in, too, aren't you?" Harry didn't answer. Applebaum prodded him, "Where you gonna go? Nobody cares about you 'cept us. You're in." Harry said nothing, but Applebaum took that for assent. "Harry's in," he repeated confidently.

"Rosie?" questioned Beeker.

"Ice cream," said Rosie. "You got to let us eat ice cream this time. And no C rations." Beeker nodded. "And fuck the beach, I guess," said the black man, with a reluctant grin.

For the next month it seemed that the whole farm had been plowed up into one enormous construction site. Contractors, electricians, all kinds of hired men found themselves in a frenzy of work. It was odd, though, when these men came to talk among themselves, how they'd all been hired from different places. Some of them had come down from St. Louis, or up from New Orleans, from Jackson, Mississippi, and Miami, Oklahoma. They couldn't find any of their number actually from Shreveport. And when something was needed immediately from the town, it was the Indian, or one of the Indian's friends, who went to get it. Nothing was said outright, but it was understood among the workers that this was a project that wasn't supposed to be known about in the immediate area. And when the men considered what they were getting paid, what with travel allowances, and overtime, and just plain old bonuses, nobody talked at all.

They were crazy, these people, but they paid in cash. And men with that kind of cash couldn't be totally out of their heads.

It was strange, though, to see that Indian kid walking around the farm with the big white Stetson on. It made his head seem tiny in comparison. Probably that other Indian was the kid's father, must be. But all those five men seemed to want to take care of the kid in one way or another. They all seemed proud of him.

The job was hellish. The architect who directed them insisted on absurdly extravagant amounts of reinforced concrete. Some of the men became convinced they were building nothing less than the ultimate survival fortress for a bunch of Armageddon freaks.

The electrician's assistants came to the other men with tales of how much wiring was going into the place. These scattered concrete buildings twenty miles from nowhere were being set up with enough power outlets to run the Astrodome. Not only were they increasing the lines from town, they were setting up generators, and a man had arrived the day before to do scouting for the best sites for a series of electricity-generating windmills. An electronic security system more elaborate and advanced than any of them had ever heard of was being set up with more than a hundred outposts along the perimeter of the property. But hell, what was out in this godforsaken place that anybody would want? Or that these men would need to protect?

"Quantum weirdness," somebody called it. The workers who had been hired on looked at the money these five strange men were putting into the house, all the extras in terms of construction and detailing, but what were they going to end up with for themselves? Six dinky bedrooms without even proper windows, just baffled air vents. Six minuscule rooms with cinder-block walls, like at a cheap state college. A locker room, and a group shower—just one bathroom for all six.

Then somebody pointed out the obvious.

It was a barracks.

One man repeated his assertion that they were a pack of rabid survivalists.

Another said that they were a bunch of guys who struck it rich, abandoned their wives, and decided to relive their fucking army experiences. He confidently predicted that six months after spending all this dough, they'd pack in it and go back home.

A third man, who probably spoke for the greatest number of the workers, said these guys could do anything they goddamn well pleased as long as they continued to pay double scale.

Beeker knew about the workers' speculations. He didn't give out false stories, however, he just let them wonder. They would have known if he had lied, and that would have made them just that much more curious. Let them figure out their own explanations.

One part of the project, however, was kept totally secret. It was a simple structure, set into the ground deep in the woods behind the clearing where the house and outbuildings were being

40

constructed. Applebaum himself had blasted the hole for it, and the first workers had filled in the concrete shell. Its wiring and plumbing were quickly done on a Saturday and Sunday by workers brought in from Birmingham. They were sent back as soon as they were finished, and never even saw the regular men. Beeker gave it out that he had changed his mind on this place, and had decided to abandon it.

The Black Berets worked on it at night, after the workers had gone home. It was a primitive bunker. Only a foot of its upper wall showed above the inclining ground on one side, and this was disguised as the base of a small, operating smokehouse. The entrance to the bunker was through a trap in the floor of the smokehouse.

It was small. A few bare cots with folded blankets at the foot were the principal furniture. It had two chairs and a long desk set up to hold a remote station of the computer that would control the security of the whole farm.

The bunker was a sunken fortress.

It was the fulfillment of Billy Leaps's vow that Tsali would never be left defenseless again. Alone, in this room, with an adjacent room filled with supplies, Tsali could hold out against Parkes and a hundred of Parkes's men—even supposing that the attackers were able to find the thing.

In five weeks, everything was done. Beeker somewhat formally shook hands with all the workers before they returned to their homes in half a dozen states. Even before the last man had driven out of sight, Cowboy rubbed his hands together and said, "Okay, Beak, time to do a little furniture shopping."

Billy Leaps looked surprised.

"What you want us to do? Spend a quarter of a million on a three-room house and a fucking barn, and then sit on the son-of-a-bitchin' floor?"

Beeker had bought a couple of new pickups, so he and Cowboy drove those down to a Montgomery Ward in a mall. Cowboy and Tsali went through and picked out things: a couple of long couches, a few chairs and small tables, a long table with six chairs to eat at, a few standing lamps. Nothing fancy, nothing that was going to break if it got knocked over a couple of times.

"All right, Beeker," said Cowboy, as he paid an astonished clerk in hundred-dollar bills, "you want to start loading up, or are you gonna help Tsali and me pick out the TV?"

"TV?" yelled Beeker, loudly enough for everybody in three aisles to turn around and stare. "I'm not having some monster TV in my house."

"Boy's gotta have a TV," said Cowboy, putting his arm around Tsali's shoulder. "What kind of boy doesn't get to watch football on a color TV? A big color TV? Like one of those things they got in bars? Wouldn't that be great?" Cowboy demanded of Tsali.

Tsali nodded uncertainly, then shook his head uncertainly.

"He doesn't need that shit," said Beeker. "Why you think we live out where we do? So I can spend another thousand dollars to bring all that shit way out there? I'm gonna teach Tsali how to shoot. You're gonna teach him how to fly that Beechcraft . . ."

"Marty's gonna teach him how to blow things apart," Cowboy grinned.

"He doesn't need—"

"Beeker, now listen. I have stood by and I have let you have your way on every fucking thing on this project." He drew Beeker aside, and spoke so that no one would overhear. "We got a house that the entire Louisiana National Guard couldn't take in a frontal assault. We got electronic equipment coming in that's so sophisticated we don't even know what it does. We got Applebaum happy as a pig in shit 'cause he is finally getting all the explosives he's ever wanted, and he's gonna pile 'em up, and sit on the very top with his arms crossed, grinnin'. We got that bunker that could withstand an atom bomb that was propped up against the door. We got it all. Except we ain't got a big color TV. Now you want to say it's not for Tsali. Fine. It ain't. It's for fucking me! I am gonna buy the biggest fucking color television in this whole fucking Montgomery Ward and you're gonna stop giving me grief about it. That's what's gonna happen."

Cowboy got his way.

That night they all sat down at the long dining table that Beeker and Cowboy had bought and loaded into the back of the pickup. The house looked good, even though it still stank of new

42

paint and still had traces of sawdust and plaster in the air. Beeker hadn't liked giving up his wood construction—a man *ought* to live in a house built of wood, because wood was a living, breathing thing. Concrete was a corpse, but it protected in a way wood did not.

Tsali was the one most impressed with the purchases of the day, not because the furniture or the appliances for the kitchen were elegant, but because they were *new*. They had been bought directly out of a store, bought with cash. Cowboy had pointed at something and said "I want that," and Cowboy had taken it away with him. There was something joyful in that, Tsali felt. In the power to do that.

But what impressed him most about this new house was the fact that he had been given his own room. He hadn't admitted it, not even to Billy Leaps, but he had never had a room of his own before. The orphanage and all the foster homes had piled kids in together. Rarely had he had a bed to himself, or a blanket, or even a pillow. Privacy was a concept that had never had a reality to Tsali before. The idea that he would have his room, that it had been given to him by the men, made him hope with just a little more confidence that his dream might come true. That he might be able to remain here, in this place, with these men.

He also took pleasure in the thought that his room was exactly like theirs, in shape and size and location. All six cubicles were lined up on the north and protected side of the house, three quarters buried in the earth. The rooms were so much alike that they had been assigned almost haphazardly—except that Applebaum was given the one at the end, farthest away from anybody, and that Harry was given the room next to his friend, because nobody else would have slept there, so close to crazy Marty.

Tsali didn't realize that Billy Leaps stared at him all through the evening meal. The older man watched Tsali rush around and try to do everything possible for their comfort. It would take time for the kid to realize that he wasn't on trial. But it was one of those things he'd have to learn, another lesson—but this would be a pleasant one. Beeker wished he could explain to the kid, but it was something Tsali would have to realize for himself. You can't just tell people things like that. They don't understand it till they feel it. Besides, when the papers came through . . .

Damn! but Beeker hoped that wouldn't be a mess. He had debated for days about it. If he just left well enough alone, the state and county officials probably wouldn't even notice that a sixteen-year-old Indian kid—handicapped at that—hadn't been in their hair for a while. But Tsali needed—Beeker needed—something more than that. Beeker wanted to adopt the kid. Tsali belonged here, with Beeker, and with the other men. And Beeker knew that the boy, who had spent his whole life under the guardianship of the welfare authorities, wouldn't ever feel safe, and at home, unless it were legal.

Beeker knew that, but he knew something else as well. He knew that the boy could never go back into the rest of the world after what he had done. Here, on the farm, with the Black Berets, Tsali was among men who understood such things as honor and battle and being warriors. But out there . . .

No one would have understood what the boy had done to Parkes's three men, why, or even how. His battle experience meant that Tsali, just as the rest of them, was now irrevocably a member of the warrior caste. Even if he never killed again. He would have to stay here with them always. There was no option. None.

Beeker would work it out somehow. The adoption would go through. It had to.

In the meantime, Tsali and Beeker and the others could relax a little bit. The house was built. What few things weren't here yet would arrive soon. He could start Tsali's lessons with the rifle. He would help the boy to get a driver's license, and then he'd let Cowboy teach him how to fly a plane. Both Beeker and Tsali would have to learn to use the telecomputer so they could communicate the next time Beeker went into the field.

All these things had to be started. Soon. They had to get going. Soon. They had to get Parkes. The sooner the better.

6

The waiting was terrible.

It was another way they realized that they were a combat team again—because of the waiting. Waiting made you nervous. Waiting drew out your strength ounce by ounce. Waiting dulled your mind and lulled your reflexes to sleep. If you let it. Except you couldn't let it.

The house was built, the fields couldn't be plowed till spring, Beeker didn't seem to be able to come up with any training exercise that even winded them, much less one that actually stretched them.

The only relief the men had from the anxious boredom was the time they spent with Tsali. They ran the boy ragged. Applebaum gave him his first lessons in demolition, and it was the only time anybody had ever heard Applebaum, aloud, express respect for the weapons he employed. Cowboy took the boy up in the plane every day, though knowing that—because of his inability to speak—he'd never be granted a license. There were times, however, when it might be crucial for a man to know how to fly a plane; and everybody knew that not every pilot in the air had a bona fide, unexpired license. Billy Leaps demanded an hour on the rifle range every day without fail, no matter what the weather. Even Rosie, the one who had known all along how easily a kid might kill, gave the boy first-aid instruction, and showed him how to drive the pickup over any sort of ground imaginable.

Tsali was exhausted from all the attention and his own responsibilities in the upkeep of the house. But he never complained. He did not know when the Black Berets might go away again. But when he was once more left alone, he wanted to be better prepared than he had been the last time. He had had luck—he knew that—on his first three kills. He wanted the ones that came after to succeed because of his skill.

Teaching the kid was the only thing that made the Black Berets feel useful. They were waiting. They were tired of waiting. It exhausted them the way a twenty-mile forced march couldn't anymore. They wanted something to do, but even more than that, they wanted Parkes.

The endless telephone calls proved useless. Billy Leaps got hold of one of the few Agency men he trusted, Frank Syms, an old hand from Saigon days. Syms had a middle-sized post at Langley, CIA headquarters. He returned Beeker's call on a safe phone and told the Cherokee that Parkes was definitely not part of Agency operations anymore. But he couldn't say more. Or wouldn't, Beeker thought.

Applebaum had plumbed his "buddies" across the country. Crazy men like himself, they all seemed to know one another. They were the ones most likely to be recruited for any mercenary activity going on. None of them knew anything about a man called Parkes or an operation called Prometheus.

The waiting went on.

They were bulls at the gate, crazed for open space and blood. The Black Berets' most cherished values—as individual men and as a team—had been violated by the raid on Laos. They had been tricked and suckered. The only good thing about the operation was that, because of it, they were together again as a team. Moreover, they were a team with a goal. They had a target. But they couldn't find him.

It reminded them of the scouting missions in 'Nam. Every scrap of intelligence, every bit of common sense told the men that there were Charlies out there in the jungle, and they'd go after the enemy. But they'd search uselessly, finding nothing. Only later would they learn that there were vast networks of caverns and caves, with laboriously dug tunnels connecting them, under the ground they tread so lightly upon. The Charlies, holding their breaths below, had been able to count them by the footsteps. Charlie was always there, but you couldn't see him when he was hiding grave-deep under the ground.

That memory made them nervy. It aroused their suspicion of everyone. They'd be on combat alert whenever they went into

46

Shreveport, always leaving one man in the back of the pickup with a few M-16s wrapped in a blanket so they wouldn't rattle. They eyed every store clerk, every gas-station attendant, every hitchhiker along the road, waiting for the telltale movement that would signal an attack. Parkes could have his own system of tunnels and caves going, for all they knew. He had sent one group of men to attack the farm, there might well be another coming.

The strength of the new house wasn't enough, not enough to give these men the sense of confidence they needed. Billy Leaps's decision to set up a system of sentries to augment the electronic surveillance just installed was accepted as a proper move by all of them. Two men were awake and ready at all times during the night, while the others slept.

The waiting went on.

Waiting, they remembered from 'Nam, had a peculiar dynamic to it. It never ended. You waited and you waited and you thought, *Something's going to happen by the time I count to ten—one two three four* . . . But you got to ten and you waited some more. And when something did happen, it happened so suddenly, and with such mind-blowing force, that you forgot that there had ever been such a thing as waiting. So, in a strange way, waiting never ended. When you were waiting, more waiting time stretched out into infinity on either side. You had waited for an eternity, you were waiting now, you would wait forever.

Parkes consumed their conversation. Every man had devised a way to kill him. Rosie wanted it slow. A couple of days, maybe. Cowboy was for a simple execution, a curt "You deserve to die for what you've done," and a bullet in the brain. This was restraint on Cowboy's part, because he'd been Parkes's particular dupe. He'd been the one who sent a bullet into Cao Dinh and cut short the life of a man who had fought beside the Black Berets in war. Cowboy had murdered a friend for Parkes. Harry just said that if he caught Parkes, he'd turn him over to Rosie, and watch.

Applebaum said he wouldn't stop with Parkes. He wanted the whole goddamn operation. He wanted to blow up offices with bombs. He wanted to toss cluster grenades into barracks. He wanted to detonate ammunition supplies, and in the end, he wanted to tie Parkes himself to a thousand-pounder and drop him from a height of two thousand feet onto a concrete slab. He wanted people in five states finding pieces of Parkes on their front lawns with the morning paper.

It didn't seem such a bad idea.

Beeker wanted Parkes most of all. It was Beeker who had a vision of what this team was. The men sat around and knew they wanted to be with one another, knew they were a team that could work. Beeker knew more. He knew they were a fighting force that could be unleashed on the world at a single command. With their resources, their courage, their experience, they could devastate any target they went after. Their stealth and ability and speed without any of the constraints of a government overseer or military chain of command was something that had to be controlled. Had to be.

They needed a general. They had to find a way to direct this awesome power for some decent purpose. Beeker knew his own limitations. After all, hadn't he—because of his great desire to have the team together again—allowed them to be duped by Parkes? That Parkes had misused such an arsenal, that he had misdirected such a power, was the thing that could never, ever be forgiven.

They wanted Parkes. Badly.

They never expected they'd get him with the help of perfumed stationery. But as soon as Billy Leaps Beeker smelled the heavy aroma of the envelope that came without a return address on it, he knew that something was going to break. No signature followed the computer-generated message inside. Beeker didn't need it. Delilah had come through.

> He's set up a staging camp in the Sahara, 125 km south of Tripoli, Libya. Under the name Resurgam, his operation is aimed at some unknown country in Africa. He has to be stopped. Be our guest.

It wasn't an offer they were about to turn down.

Beeker called an immediate council of war. He used the new communications system to call Cowboy down from the air. His excitedly barked orders brought Rosie and Applebaum in from the perimeter where they'd been checking the new surveillance system. Harry was already with him.

Cowboy brought the plane down with as much speed as he had when they'd returned to find the farm a charred ruin. Only one thing could have gotten Billy Leaps as agitated as he sounded over the radio. And that was Parkes. Tsali was beside the pilot and watched with awe and some nervousness at the way the Texan dived the plane, almost as though he were purposely going to crash into the asphalt pavement. When he had brought the Beechcraft to a halt outside its hangar—almost miraculously, it seemed—Cowboy turned to Tsali and said crisply, "Don't you ever do it that way, kid." Tsali shook his head and agreed.

The others sat in the living room of the house, each man tense with excitement, waiting for Cowboy to come through the door. Beeker started to speak as soon as the pilot had taken his seat.

He read the letter aloud and let the message sink in. "Rosie," he said at last, "this is a setup for you."

"Me?"

"Yeah. They're going to Africa. You can put on your best liberation-front bullshit—if you can remember how it goes—and get in on it."

"What you want me to do, walk across the Sahara Desert till I find the fucking place? 'Start at the Pyramids and go west' or something?" the big black demanded. "Beeker, I don't know where that camp is, nobody does probably. We just got this four-line message and that's all."

Beeker realized he had gone too quickly. He took a breath and explained, "They must be mercs if they're going into Africa. They have to be forming an army. This isn't some little raid, doesn't look like. So all we have to do is get in on it. Rosie, you'll be first. Applebaum, you can go too. You're both the types to jump in with both feet on something like this. Rosie, what you've got to do is construct a profile that the recruiter'll buy. That's where the black liberation stuff comes in." Beeker turned to Applebaum and grinned. "Marty, they'll take one look at you, and they'll *know* you're crazy."

"Yeah!" agreed Applebaum, who took it for a vast compliment.

"What if they already got their forces?" Harry asked.

"Never happens to them. They never have enough men. There's always guys fucking off who have to be replaced. Always these guys ten years out who think they want to go back, then they get one taste of discipline again, and they want to run home to their wives and five kids. Anyway, even if they were filled up, with their skills they'd take on Rosie and Marty. We just got to hope that for the time being, Parkes is not on the spot. 'Cause he might recognize some of us. But I don't think he will be. He's the type to run things from his desk, and over the telephone."

"So how do we join?" Applebaum demanded.

Beeker laughed. "Marty, you're gonna answer every single classified ad in *Soldiers' Adventures*. And we are all gonna help you."

"And me?" Rosie asked.

"Same thing. We'll send Cowboy on a scouting trip. Up to Washington." He glanced at the pilot. Cowboy smiled broadly, his *I'm gonna get laid* grin. Billy Leaps knew exactly how to deal with that. "I'm going to call some of my friends from the Corps. They'll have contacts. They'll take you to all the places in D.C. and around Norfolk where the mercs hang out. You might need some help—some strong arms—and they'll give it to you."

"Hey, Beeker! No! I mean—" Cowboy had had more than enough dealings with Billy Leaps's Marine buddies to know he didn't want them around while he was in Washington. They cramped his style. "I can work better alone. I can be more mobile. I can—"

"Forget it, Cowboy, this is an assignment, it's not R&R. Those guys I'm sending you to will know more about what's going on than most intelligence people. You know how merc types flock to Marines."

"Like fleas to a mangy bird dog," said Cowboy dismally. Merc types clung to Marines, and Marines clung to their assignments. He'd be in Washington, but he doubted if he'd even get to telephone Karole. Though, hell, he didn't care about *talking* to her. He just wanted—

"Now," said Beeker, his commanding voice dispelling the dream, "let's get out the magazines, get the ads answered. And Harry"—he turned to the enormous, extraordinarily hairy Greek man who was so often quiet, even among them—"you got some business in Chicago?"

Harry shrugged. "I guess I ought to see about closing down the bar. If it's still there. Now that we're staying together. Maybe . . ." He trailed off.

Harry had thought for a while of opening another place in Shreveport, but why the hell should he bother with that? He didn't need the trouble, he didn't need the abuse, he didn't even need the money. The Black Berets were back together, and it looked as if they were going to be together for a long, long time. There was no need for a bar, and there was no one else Harry had to take care of but Harry. And Marty, maybe, just a little bit.

Billy Leaps waited a few moments for the Greek to go on, but when it was obvious Harry wasn't going to say anything else, Beeker advised, "As long as you're there, do a little scouting. May be something going on at Great Lakes." Great Lakes—thirty miles north of Chicago—was where Harry'd got his Navy SEAL training. He'd know a few of the drill sergeants at Great Lakes, those seasoned veterans who got tired of training a bunch of teen-agers to become amphibious shock troops, useless in a peacetime force. These drill sergeants were fodder for the mercenary recruiters, just the kind of restless men who'd take an assignment for the excitement as much as for the money.

"I can check it out," Harry said.

Beeker nodded his head sharply. "You got business, Marty?" he asked Applebaum. The blond man blushed with sudden embarrassment. He didn't want to admit this, but he supposed he had to.

"Yeah, I got to say good-bye to my mother." Even though no one laughed, Applebaum's wan face reddened even more after the acknowledgment.

"Do it. In Jersey?" Applebaum nodded, yes. "You can check out some places around Fort Dix."

Beeker then turned to the black man. "Rosie? You don't have any business, do you?"

Rosie looked at Beeker and shook his head. There was no wife. She had left years ago. There were no children. Never would be, now. Parents long dead. No house. When Beeker had come to fetch him, he had been living in a rented room. Landlady probably pawned his clothes and his other junk months ago. Friends? They were all in this room. No, he didn't have any business.

51

7

Applebaum proved invaluable in answering the ads in the magazines. There were a dozen of them on the newsstands. Each of them appealed to the macho bravado of American men, offering them sharp and pointed memories of those times when they had had a moment of true masculinity and comradeship, in the uniform of their country.

American men are forced into domesticity. The most use they get from their muscles is pushing a lawnmower. The only opportunity they have to measure their technical strength is fighting a traffic jam.

Men are supposed to do, and to be, more than that. They weren't born to live in wifely-neat houses in manicured suburbs or to fight petty battles with neighbors pettier than themselves. So these men, who have felt their virility dribbling away, returned in their minds to their years in the service, the few months of their lives when they had been challenged as men are supposed to be challenged, as hunters, fighters, warriors. They nurtured those dreams, and dreamed of another such opportunity. When the chances didn't present themselves they turned to the magazines that gave their memories shape and detail. The articles reminded them of the feel and the smell of their field arms, the delirious excitement of combat, the thrilling challenge and satisfactions of mere survival in battle.

The magazines went one further. They offered the bravest more than a dream of returning. Articles on mercenary operations were invariably included, tales of American men who still fought in exotic countries and terrains, who slept under the stars in foreign fields. The technical articles, the life histories, and the fantastical exploits of these soldiers-of-fortune combined to re-mind American males that there were still ways to be men.

The fantasy wouldn't be so potent, if there weren't a dollop of reality added. The advertisements in the classified pages of the magazines did that. Some of them were even real, thinly veiled inducements for men to join the real mercenary armies that still battled around the world. There were still wars to be fought and still a need for professional soldiers to fight them.

The P.O. box numbers were the recruiters. Men who could give substance to the restless American man's dream of combat.

The Black Berets clipped all the ads and started to answer them. But they—real fighters, true warriors—discovered they didn't know the words to describe what they had learned over the course of hundreds of real battles, small and large. They didn't know how to describe themselves, probably the greatest and most effective team to fight in the entire course of the Vietnam War. But Applebaum, always ready to crow about his combat experience and, like a bantam rooster, always ready to fight without thinking about the worth of the prize—Applebaum knew the words.

"Hardassed combat vet wants blood. Will travel. Have gun. Need combat."

Even though he was talking to the others on the team, men who had known him for years, could weigh his capabilities and his deficiencies to the quarter ounce, Applebaum strutted and postured as though he were showing off in a college-town bar.

"Need the taste of blood," he snarled, as if Cowboy, taking down his words, could get the snarl in there too. "My tattoo says it all. *I BRING DEATH.*"

Beeker said they could get along with just three or four replies by repeating them in different letters, but Applebaum insisted on a different one for every ad. The others marveled at his imagination in coming up with them, each more grandiose in its promises than the last.

"The most feared fighting man in the SEALs seeks action to counter stateside boredom."

"Growlin', snarlin', always ready Navy vet looking for action. No pussy-face security forces need reply."

Though Applebaum was perfectly serious through this—for

once he was able to say aloud exactly how he liked to think about himself—Rosie started to laugh. Beeker shook his head warningly.

"You're doing fine, Marty," he said. "Keep going." Beeker knew that Applebaum's wildly exaggerated descriptions of themselves and their actual bloody experience in Vietnam would be more convincing than anything else they could have come up with.

Each response had an introduction inspired by one of Applebaum's dictations. Then each man compiled a full résumé of skills. Beeker reminded the men not to make them look too professional. The applications should be legible, but not necessarily clean and nice. "You're not applying for a job at Allstate Insurance."

They addressed all the envelopes and for a measure of excitement used Express Mail to get them all delivered the next day. The answers would come quickly.

Then Harry—always weary Harry—climbed on a commercial jet to fly to Chicago to take care of his business. Cowboy took Applebaum with him as far as Washington—though not without protest, dreading the hours alone in the air with only Marty for company. "He's the only one-man riot I ever knew up close," Cowboy complained. Beeker sent Rosie down to New Orleans to pick up certain supplies he didn't want purchased in the immediate neighborhood. Billy Leaps himself remained on the farm with Tsali, and his waiting began again.

Cowboy sat in the bar near the Marine barracks in Washington. He was groaning. But not from pain. From the frustration of it all. Here he was, just a few miles from Karole, and who was he with? Jarheads. Crazed damned jarheads. Billy Leaps's network of Marines was something that Cowboy had encountered often. With a word the leatherneck network went into action and moved to act for their own.

Fucking Marines!

Give them an assignment and it's all they could think about. No number of beautiful women, no drugs, no diversion of any kind would stop these near-automatons once they were set in motion.

Find some mercenaries, Beeker had said. And that's what Cowboy's honor guard was about to do. Their friend, the Cherokee, wanted to know who was hiring mercs; they'd find out for him.

And Cowboy would have the privilege of accompanying them on their rounds.

These guys must get laid, Cowboy knew it. They had to get laid. They talked about getting laid as much as Applebaum did. But could he get them to take just an hour, a quick hour in the early evening, to go over to where Karole worked so they could scout up some playtime? Oh no, they were on assignment from their friend Billy Leaps Beeker. They couldn't do *that*.

Bunch of fucking Boy Scouts!

There were two of them with Cowboy this time. Sergeant Harry Rembaud, a Cajun happy to meet someone else from Louisiana, was one.

"I'm from Texas!" Cowboy screamed.

"Live in Shreveport now," the big man with the dark skin, nearly as dark as Beeker's, had answered. "Shreveport's always been in Louisiana before. Maybe you just got some sense and left Texas."

Cowboy groaned at the insult, but the pain of his injured Texas pride was nothing compared to the frustration he felt knowing that Karole was only three blocks away.

The other one was in the Reserves. You had to watch out for Marine Reserves. It was bad enough when the guys are in the Corps, but when they go home and you deprive them of their day-to-day contact with other Marines they get crazy. They become obsessed. Sergeant Tully Jenks was like that. You could tell the days and nights he got to go on Reserve duty or help out a buddy like Beeker were like Days of Holy Obligation to him. They were the moments that he was raised up out of the mire of his pedestrian life and was able to feel that he was still a Marine.

Tully Jenks was stone-faced. He didn't laugh at Cowboy's jokes or take any interest in Cowboy's stories. He certainly didn't pay any attention to Cowboy's complaints. Tully Jenks was on assignment.

The assignment had taken them from bar to bar in this section of town, close to the embassies, closer to the Marine barracks. They had made inquiries, they had asked questions, they had probed vague leads. Nothing came of it. "There'll never be anything," Cowboy thought.

But on about Cowboy's eighth bourbon of the evening, Tully

Jenks nudged him and jerked his head to the right. Cowboy looked in that direction. An Arab-looking man stood nearby, obviously staring at the table. He approached, not hesitantly, but with slow deliberation.

"I believe you gentlemen have been making some investigations," he said in a formal English, obviously educated, just as obviously not his native language. "Perhaps I can be of some service."

"I fucking hope so," returned Cowboy. If he couldn't get to Karole, at least he could accomplish his part of the job and go home. God knows, it was more fun being out in the middle of the forest on that farm, going up every day with Tsali, than it was sitting here in the middle of one of the world's great capitals. At least at the farm he didn't have a pair of goddamned Marine baby-sitters on either side of him all the time.

Fucking Marines!

Applebaum was in a bar as well, something called the Stars and Stripes. It was near Fort Dix and it advertised strippers in neon. He was downing one beer after another, even though it didn't do any good. Though Applebaum was small, alcohol had no appreciable effect on him, even after a long evening of steady consumption. Drugs didn't either, for that matter.

But he was drinking now, and drinking in hope that he would feel the deadening effect of the alcohol. He was pissed. Furious. Goddamn why did he always come home? There was no reason to. It never got any better.

It would never get better because Marty would never be a doctor, or a dentist, or a lawyer. He'd never own a chain of anything. He'd never give his mother a daughter-in-law to complain about or grandchildren she could boast over. She'd always accused him of being a vagabond, a good-for-nothing with no self-discipline. It was bad enough, she said, that he always managed to ruin his own life, but on top of everything else, he was setting a bad example for his two younger brothers. After his mother's divorce, Martin Applebaum had become the man of the family, but to Marty's mother, it looked like he was turning out even worse than his father. Marty's father had been no prize, but at least he had had a job, a real job, and had managed to buy a house for his family.

And so on, and so on. It went on forever. It never changed at all. Nothing Marty could do was right, and nothing his two younger brothers had ever done was wrong. One of them owned a shoe store in a New Jersey mall. The other taught at a private boys' school in Vermont. Both were married, both had children, both had nice houses, and went to temple sometimes, and sent nice presents for Hanukkah, and called home once a week no matter what.

This time he went back, and he brought his mother a diamond necklace. Real diamonds held in place with real gold.

"How much did it cost?" she asked him.

He told her. It was more than his brothers, together, made in a year.

"Where did you get the money?" she asked him.

He couldn't tell her.

"Gangster," she accused him. "You're a gangster now." She put the necklace on and, standing before the mirror, turned her head this way and that to see how she looked in it. "Gangster," she said. "I won't wear a gangster's presents."

"Then give it back," said Marty.

"No," she said, glaring at him through the reflection in the mirror, "you gave it to me. I'm going to put it in the safe-deposit box, and it will go to your brothers' children. I hope they never find out their uncle is a gangster."

In the Stars and Stripes, Martin Applebaum stared at his face in the mirror behind the bar, and said over and over through clenched teeth, "I am not. I am not."

"What aren't you, punk? A man?" The big guy to his right said that. The big guy was one of four. They were in civilian clothes, but it was obvious they would have been much more at home in khaki. They might as well have had *Fort Dix* tattooed on the foreheads. Sergeant, a corporal, and two privates. Calm, an expression of complete inner peace came into Marty's eyes. Anyone looking into the reflection of Marty's face in the mirror at that moment would have thought it was total relaxation that he had just experienced. It was. Marty was crazy at the best of times.

Five minutes with his mother could put Marty completely over the edge—even for Marty. When it came down to it, she was the one person in the world that Marty felt he couldn't handle. But some asshole Army sergeant in a bar?

He loved it. He just ate it up when some big jerk looked at his slight frame and thought he saw an easy mark. Marty was thirty-three. He could have passed for twenty-three. Sometimes he was still carded. Everyone thought he was the original ninety-pound weakling. Until they got to know him.

Marty turned very, very slowly and faced the sergeant. He was over six feet. Fine by Marty. He looked muscular. What the hell. He had his three friends with him. Made things more interesting. Marty looked him in the eye. His own code demanded one more question. "You saying that to me?" Marty's voice was soft, even gentle.

The big man looked at Marty's five-seven frame, at the watery blue eyes behind the thick glasses, at the dirty blond hair that had frizzed in the bar's humidity. He looked ridiculous, the guy thought. Him and his friends could have a field day with this little bastard, this nerdy-looking weed, who came into a real servicemen's club, and took up space at the bar, and talked to himself as he stared into the mirror. "Yeah, I'm talking to you . . . *faggot*."

"That's it," thought Marty calmly, but already he was attempting to channel the wave of adrenaline surging through him. "That's it."

It happened quickly. Marty doubled over like a man who's suddenly realized he has a major stomach ache. Between his legs he clasped his hands, joined them to make a double fist. The sergeant was puzzled: why was the blond twerp bending over so far? He didn't even move to defend himself. Too bad. Because as Marty stepped forward, his joined hands came up in a wide, sweeping arc. Hard force, insane anger, and trained skill all combined. And they all smashed into the sergeant's testicles with a power that lifted all six feet of military brawn into the air.

But the pain! The pain was so intense that the sergeant actually doubled over in midair. By the time he fell to the floor he was already in a fetal position so tight that he didn't do anything to stop his head from bouncing on the wood. He was in such pain that he couldn't yell.

Marty didn't wait to see if the friends were going to give the guy a helping hand. A foot flared out at the redhead who had been at the big guy's right. Marty figured—and he was correct—that these men weren't prepared for what he was giving out. So he took a chance and left his own body momentarily vulnerable while his foot flew up in the air. Incredibly, it reached high enough to land against the redhead's jaw. Marty wore heavy leather boots with steel-lined toes. The jaw dislocated with a grinding and shattering of bone.

Two remained. But they reacted faster. They had their hands up in a defensive posture. "Hey, man, I never saw these dudes before in my life," claimed the black one. He was lying, they were his platoon mates, but he wasn't going to let this crazy man know that. Not unless he had the whole platoon with him. Maybe not even then. The other one—a Latino—made the same vows of disloyalty.

"Get their carcasses out of my sight."

"Yes, sir," the two others said, and quickly dragged away the two injured men. One was unconscious from the blow to his jaw, and the sergeant whimperingly begged someone to take away the pain in his nuts.

Marty turned to his beer, still sweating on the cork coaster, and waited for someone to come up. Sometimes it was the women. They always came after a fight, as if blood and violence were a part of their foreplay. He loved them best, the fawning ones, the ones who wanted a warrior's prick. Sometimes, particularly Stateside, it was a bouncer who got there ahead of the girls. He wondered who it would be tonight.

It wasn't the girls or the bouncer. Instead, he got a dark, tanned man who handed him a card reading *International Security Association*. Shit, he had wanted a piece of ass. He had needed a piece of ass. It took him a while, and a lot of reinforcement, to recover from a bout with his mother. But the tanned man in the anonymous brown clothing said, "You want a job?"

He might be a lead, Marty thought. And Beeker'll kill me if I pass up a lead. "Let's talk," said Marty, and carried his beer over to an empty booth.

8

It didn't take Harry long to unload the bar. He had a cousin who'd always wanted to buy in with him. He told the cousin to find a lawyer to draw up the papers the next day. Both the cousin and the attorney were shocked to see the disdain with which Harry dealt with the whole business.

He had a single answer for every question that was asked him: "I don't care." It was true. Whenever he was away from the team, whenever he wasn't in combat or preparing for combat or resting up from combat, Harry didn't care much about things. "Do what's easiest," he told them.

He finished it all on the second day. Signed, sealed, delivered into his cousin's hands. He didn't even bother to notice when the payments were supposed to be made by his cousin. If he got the checks, he figured, he'd get the checks. If he didn't? He didn't need the money, and he certainly wasn't going to reclaim his bar on Chicago's South Side.

Harry took the train north to Great Lakes.

The little Navy town on the shore of Lake Michigan is a tawdry island of honky-tonk in the middle of one of the world's richest suburban neighborhoods. After the manicured lawns of Winnetka and the magnificent mansions of Lake Forest comes the village of Great Lakes. Great Lakes is a painted whore standing beside a Mom of the Year and a Daughter of the American Revolution. It's a strip of bars and rip-off car dealerships, barely hidden prostitution and drugs, bright lights and loud music.

Harry found Sal's easily enough. It was a little sleazier than its neighbors. No bright lights outside, a peeling sign nailed to the door, windows so grimy you couldn't see through them. Sal's had its regular clientele and didn't need to draw in the recruits who were getting their first passes. Recruits, even when they wandered into this place, didn't stay there long. It showed them too plainly what they'd become if they stayed in the Navy.

Harry knew it was the right place. A couple of phone calls and some rumors had said so. Now he knew for sure. It was in the eyes of the customers, in the attitude of the bartender. It was obvious in the way the cocktail waitresses moved about the grimy floor. *Cocktail waitresses!* It was a phrase from the fifties, a leftover from Sal's final stab at respectability. It looked as if some of the women working the floor were left over from the fifties as well. They were over-the-hill broads glad they had a place left for them in the world. They had the fortitude to stick out an entire life in a place like this—picking up their first dime and obscene proposition in one corner, and their last quarter and ass-pat in another.

They were tough ladies who had seen it all—and done it all. They weren't hooking, but there wasn't one woman working in Sal's who couldn't be had for a few bucks, if you were ready to screw someone who was sure to yawn in the middle of everything.

"Whatcha want?" one of them asked Harry after he had taken a seat in a booth on the side. The red naugahyde was stained and faded and ripped. The cotton padding boiled up out of the cushions.

He actually smiled. Something Harry almost never did. He knew her. That wasn't a great surprise. There are places like Sal's in every Navy town. A woman comfortable in one will be just as comfortable in another. "Annie," Harry said. "Annie McCameron."

She studied his face for a minute, looking at those eyes. She was trying to discover if this was just another joker claiming to have known her, or was he someone who had been important. There had been a lot of important men in Annie McCameron's life. A lot of them.

She finally remembered. Vietnam. How could she forget? But then, there had been so many men she had known there. She spoke his name, "Harry," with almost a sigh. Yeah, this one had been important.

She turned to the barkeep. "Tony, two double scotches. I'm taking my break."

Annie sat down across from Harry. Her face was hard, and even the dim light of Sal's showed sadness in her eyes almost as great as the sadness in his own.

"Why Great Lakes, Annie? Had you pegged for the big time."

"Couldn't take the city, Harry. Tired of the big base towns. Had a place in San Diego. My own place. Then got mixed up with a man—you know how it is for me—and I lost it. Him too. Course, I still had my nest egg." Even when she was desperately in love, Annie always maintained a few bank accounts spread out over the map. She didn't give up their numbers to anybody. It was a trick "cocktail waitresses" learned from one another. "So I moved on. Wasn't gonna give up the military, but I wanted a small place. Not much going on. A little quiet. I knew some guys stationed here and I figured it'd do. Got me a little house a few miles west of here. Got a garden, would you believe it? Got me a goddamn breakfast nook."

She laughed and then the laughter faded, and in the silence they both remembered old dreams.

Harry brought himself back to his assignment. He had to give Annie a cover. "I got a place too, down in Louisiana. Farm with Beeker, remember him?"

"Indian?" Annie asked. "Got his ear shot off somewhere?"

"Khe Sanh," said Harry. Goddamn, everything brought up memories. "Anyway, we got a farm down there. Nice place. But it's getting to me, Annie. I need a change of pace. Got to go back to something that'll get the juices flowing."

"That why you're here? Reenlisting?"

"I'm too old for training games. I need—"

He broke off, and sipped his scotch. Annie signaled for two more.

"You need what?" she asked.

"You know what I need," said Harry quietly. "Some action."

"Some guys gotta go back." She looked up at him over the rim of her glass. "You one of them guys, Harry?"

"Yeah. Can you understand that, Annie?"

Annie grinned mirthlessly. "You're asking me? When you're sitting with me in a dump like this? You're asking me if I know that people do what they got to do?"

"I guess you know," said Harry.

"Sure I do. All my life, that's what I've done. What I had to do. And I haven't done nothing else. And right now I gotta go." JoAnn, the other waitress, brought two more scotches. Annie stood up, took the glass from the waitress, and downed it in one gulp. Looking down at Harry, she said in an expressionless, almost cold voice, "Good to see you, Harry. When you leave tonight, leave your number with Tony. Give me a couple of days. I'll let you know who's hiring."

With that, Annie was gone. But she kept her promise.

9

They all came back on the same day. Cowboy had picked up Applebaum in New Jersey and suffered through an endlessly detailed story about the fight in the Fort Dix bar. When Cowboy accused Applebaum of exaggerating, Applebaum simply retaliated with more details. The worst part of Applebaum's stories—other than the length—was that he always added sound effects. Sound effects made the story even longer, and gave all Applebaum's fights and battles a comic-book quality. All the way back, Cowboy wondered if he and the team wouldn't be better off if Applebaum accidentally fell out of the plane. Over a granite quarry in Virginia, say. Or a plowed field in Georgia. Without a parachute. They might need his demolition skills, though. They had before. Cowboy flicked a little switch in his brain to turn off his ears.

By the time they landed at the farm, Harry had already returned. Beeker had fetched him at the airport that morning.

Beeker, for his part, had made everything ready here on the farm. The loot from Laos meant they could afford some fancy dealing. Each man had been given a different telephone number to hand out. Through a little Ma Bell magic Cowboy had picked up from some of his coke customers who were phone freaks as well, the people who placed the calls wouldn't even know they were phoning Shreveport. Beeker didn't want anyone to pinpoint a group of mercenaries suddenly rising out of the Louisiana backwoods. People calling Cowboy thought he was back in Houston. Those trying to reach Applebaum were deluded into thinking they were reaching Miami. But the telephone that rang would be the black six-button set next to Billy Leaps's chair.

All five men had been provided fake histories ready for use.

Harry had made sure that Annie did not give away his true name when she made contact for him. It didn't matter though—it was unlikely even Annie would have remembered a name like Haralambos Georgeos Pappathannassiou. Beeker had even used his Marine network to reach into the Pentagon computers and produce 214s for all the men under false names. Everything was ready. Even if Parkes himself was running the recruiting operation he'd never recognize the names. The service records themselves were changed just enough so that anyone who knew the Black Berets personally wouldn't match them up with the faked identities.

Rosie's call came first, one of the *Soldiers' Adventures* responses that Applebaum had fired off. Rosie played the black militant role to the hilt. He answered the phone with his cover name, "Abdul Muhamed." So as not to distract the black man, the others sat back very still, but they watched and listened intently. Rosie was silent for more than two minutes, hearing out the spiel.

"I will not play the stooge for some white man's exploitation of the black peoples of Africa," Rosie suddenly cried out in a booming voice. "I will not pledge my Islamic sword to forces that would overwhelm the freedom of Africa!"

Applebaum became convulsed with silent laughter. Beeker stood up suddenly, and would have lunged for Marty, but Harry got there first. He swiped out his hand, and pressed Applebaum against the back of the chair hard.

On and on Rosie's conversation went. By the time the call was over the merc recruiter must have thought he had found the most radical black freedom fighter to rise up since Huey Newton.

Rosie set up an appointment for himself. When he hung up the phone he turned and grinned at the rest of them. "New York City, and I'm supposed to get there ready to move out!"

The Black Berets cheered. The plan was working.

Rosie's was only the first of several calls that day. Some were from security agencies, and these were quickly disposed of. Others were from men whose motive in placing the ads in the magazine was merely for the chance to talk to such men as the Black Berets on the telephone, and ask them about their exploits. "There's a bunch of really sick people out there," said Applebaum in disgust, after he slammed down the phone on the second of these calls. But one by one, that day and the next, the men made their contacts. All but Billy Leaps. He'd arrive later, alone. Without an invitation.

"What if it's not the right one? The right operation?" Cowboy demanded. "What if you send us off on four different missions? Four different jobs that don't have nothing to do with Prometheus, or Parkes?"

"The money's the same. The dates are the same. It's a lot of recruiting taking place at one time," Billy Leaps answered. "Somebody's in a hurry. And I'm willing to take a bet on who that somebody is."

Beeker was right. It was all the same operation. Rosie was the first to discover that. He had taken a commercial flight to New York and gone immediately to the assigned meeting place. Not a bar, no dive for this operation. They were obviously trying to impress their potential recruits with their status and resources. The operation had offices in a luxury building on Fifth Avenue. The sign on the door read merely RESURGAM INC.

Rosie arrived wearing a dashiki to underline his freedom-fighter cover. But in the bitter New York winter weather he surely did wish he had his uniform thermals instead—those and a good heavy Army issue jacket. But image was everything. He'd keep up the image.

The guy who greeted him from behind the expensive-looking office door was a nerd. Rosie knew it at once. He introduced himself to Rosie as Mac Knife. Rosie chewed on the inside of his cheek to keep from laughing. It was a good thing Applebaum wasn't around. Mac Knife. What an asshole. Image might be everything, but it wasn't necessary to carry it into caricature.

Rosie kept a stern exterior, as befitted an African warrior. He sat stony-faced on the other side of the desk, and measured the rap. Mac Knife—tall but skinny, pale in sharp contrast to his almost black hair—laid out a rehearsed version of the trip. He knew it by rote, and rattled it off, all the time staring at the shining ivory skull that pierced the lobe of Rosie's left ear.

"Mr. . . . er . . . Muhamed," the man said, shifting uncomfortably in his swiveling chair, "there are many different positions that we will need to fill. We're looking for specialists as well as general . . . ah . . . guards.''

"Guards," Rosie echoed. "I din't hear nothin' 'bout being no guard."

Again, Rosie had to stifle a laugh. He loved doing a cotton-field accent.

Mac Knife looked over the folder he had open in front of him. Rosie knew it was a copy of his fake service record; he could see from where he sat. "I guess we can be frank. Given your extensive service in Vietnam, it's obvious you were more than a regular soldier."

"Yeah!" Rosie boomed.

Knife was staring at the earring again. "Well, ah . . ." He was having trouble with his concentration. "Yes, well, perhaps I should be more honest. Straightforward. A man like you . . ." He trailed off again. "This is a military operation. But a military operation of the greatest secrecy. It must remain confidential. I can't tell you exactly where—"

"Africa," said Rosie.

"Well . . ." Knife paused, trying to create the image of assent, without actually confirming Rosie's surmise.

You turkey, thought Rosie. *You white-meat turkey*.

"South Africa?" demanded Rosie aloud. "If you and your people are 'xpecting Abdul Muhamed—"

"No, no," said Knife quickly, "nothing to do with South Africa."

"*Against* South Africa?" Rosie smiled broadly, as though relishing the idea. "Is Abdul Muhamed gonna help crush Pretoria and the white racist supremacist government of the unlawful state what has—"

"Not against South Africa, either," said Mac Knife, a little apologetically.

"Some other white racist supremacist African state?"

"Mr. Muhamed, certainly you are aware that some of the black regimes in Africa are among the most repressive governments in the world. Some of the most cruel in the treatment of their people. Let's just say you won't find any difficulty in reconciling your political views to the aims of our particular project. I can assure you of that. In any event," Knife went on blithely, confident of having regained control of the interview, "you will be expected to act like a soldier and follow your orders."

"I follow *blind*," Rosie promised vehemently. And he meant it. As long as the orders came from Billy Leaps Beeker.

"Good. Now back to your specialties. It appears from this extraordinary record that you might have some . . . experience . . ." He looked around the room for the right phrase. He came up with ". . . experience in extracting statements and information from captured operatives."

"I give it to 'em," said Rosie stonily. The muscles of his upper arms quivered. "I give it to 'em, and then I get it out of 'em."

Rosie wondered what details the service record gave that made Knife stumble so. The man grew pale just reading the paragraphs. "Well . . . I need some sort of indication that your experience in this field is real. It's just not always possible to rely on . . ." He didn't seem to be able to finish a sentence. He tapped the service record. "These aren't always reliable, they . . ." He trailed off again with a worried look on his face, as if he didn't care to learn any more details of Mr. Abdul Muhamed's methods of extracting information. But then he gathered up courage and asked, "How would you yourself, Mr. Muhamed, go about getting information from an uncooperative captive? Away from base, and without sophisticated equipment."

Rosie grinned. His teeth glistened and he felt as though his earring had lit up like a bright city light. "I starts with his nuts. You know, easy stuff. Man don't like peoples fooling around with his nuts. Makes him uncom-fortable just thinking about it."

It was obviously making Mr. Knife uncomfortable.

"They is always passing out," Rosie went on, "when you starts foolin' around down there. So you got to go slow and easy."

Knife nodded, ashen. *Where does Parkes find them?* Rosie thought.

"The real hard ones, well, you can take a knife. See, Mr. Knife," said Rosie, taking an Al Mar lockblade out of his pocket, and opening it up with obvious relish, "then you just takes the knife and you slits 'em open. A little slice here. There.

Don't want 'em to pass out yet, you just slits open the skin nice and easy.'' He gestured casually toward the shaken white man's face, chest, arms with the knife.

"That's quite sufficient, Mr. Muhamed. You've convinced me. Totally.''

Leaving only Billy Leaps and Tsali behind, the others threw their gear into the Beechcraft. Cowboy would fly them to New Orleans to catch other planes, and then he'd return to the farm. After they hit New Orleans, Rosie, Applebaum, and the Greek would be on their own. Billy Leaps Beeker and Tsali stood outside the hangar and watched the Beechcraft lift off. After it was well into the sky, Tsali poked Billy Leaps to get his attention, to have him watch his hands while he communicated.

Will the warriors all return from this battle?

"You have to learn not to ask that question,'' Billy Leaps said patiently, slowly. "There's no answer to it. Sometimes they all do. Sometimes they don't. But I'll say this. The five of us got through Vietnam. And we got through the ten years since Vietnam. The five of us are on borrowed time. And we all know it. But we don't think about it. And you don't either, understand? You do what you're supposed to do, and that's what you think about.''

Beeker was surprised at himself, for saying so much. He had already been thinking about it, he guessed.

Will you go, too? the boy signed.

Beeker nodded. "Cowboy and I will go later. But not till we've made this base secure, and I'm sure you can handle it by yourself.''

I will pray to the gods to let you come back.

Billy Leaps Beeker looked away and pretended to scan the skies for the last sight of Cowboy's plane. Beeker had survived so much, so many battles, so many skirmishes with death, with no one at home praying for his return. Now that there was the boy, waiting for him, and praying to the gods for his safety, would Death at last grab Beeker by the collar? When it truly mattered to him that he continue to live? Billy Leaps turned to speak to the boy, but Tsali had already turned away and was walking back toward the house.

69

10

The heat in Libya was almost intense as that Rosie had experienced in Southeast Asia. But this desert heat lacked the humidity of that other place, that devastating wetness that made a man forget where his sweat ended and the air around him began. This was dry heat, easy heat for a 'Nam vet.

Roosevelt Boone, alias Mr. Abdul Muhamed, walked around the makeshift camp deep in the Libyan desert and watched the commando preparations and the newly organized terrorist training squads with hardly hidden disgust.

Rosie had just walked through every test the camp commanders could devise to test his prowess, his knowledge, and his reflexes so effortlessly that he had been told that he would help to give instruction.

The camp was run by Major Ronald Ascham, who gave the impression that he had been in the English Army. He was a sterling example of a type the Black Berets had learned to hate in 'Nam. The type who believed in John Wayne movies, who thought that since the VC weren't White Protestant North Europeans they'd lay down their arms and die of fright at the sight of American or British or Australian—or whatever—troops.

Wrong. Very, very wrong.

Rosie learned early in life that he was a follower, but that didn't mean he had to follow a fool. A man wanted Rosie's allegiance, he damned well earned it. Respect isn't given away, it's something a leader has to work for. Billy Leaps Beeker had done that. And Rosie had followed him to the ends of the world because of it. Laos was the end of the world, and Libya was the stop beyond that. But Major Asshole—it was a short and obvious step to that name from Major Ascham—Rosie wouldn't have followed Major Asshole through the front door of a ten-story whorehouse.

Major Asshole strutted through the camp. The troops gathered there for training included many women, hardened veterans of their own wars, wars that no longer acknowledged the difference in the sexes. Wars in countries that had no exports left except troops. Palestinian women who had seen family and homes blasted from underneath them—by both sides, and every mindless faction in between. South Vietnamese women who had fought the victorious Communist forces bare-handed when the gutless United States had abandoned that particular commitment because it had grown inconvenient and embarrassing. Others, too, from Afghanistan, from Cyprus, from Nigeria and Rhodesia, from a dozen troubled areas on the world map.

The camp was laid out in long parallel lines. Rosie walked up and down the carefully even streets that had been established on the outskirts of a town that had been destroyed in some skirmish twenty or thirty years ago. Parkes's underlings had brought together over three hundred fighters, men and women, white and black and brown and yellow and Irish. Rosie counted the last separately. He didn't think any racial group should have to own up to the Irish. Rosie wasn't certain yet whether all these men and women were intended for the one particular coup Parkes was aiming at, or whether he intended to keep the group together, for other missions. Time would tell.

A hundred different motives had attracted this group to the Libyan desert training ground.

Some were just out for blood, for the opportunity to indulge their one overwhelming obsession, of bringing death. This was certainly the case for the Irish girl Brenda, the one that Major Asshole was so hot for. She had red hair and blue eyes, and her skin was so painfully red and freckled from the sun that it made Rosie hurt just to look at it. But Brenda wouldn't wear a hat to protect her face; the blistering just made her that much meaner.

The Irish, the Palestinians, the Vietnamese—they were people who fought because that's what they knew about. They were apprentices in their countries' one great industry—war. They had been trained in a single skill: killing others while remaining alive

71

themselves. Rosie knew they'd be deadly enemies, for anyone. Deadly because every one of them expected to die in the field.

Then there were those who had joined up for bravado, the armchair soldiers who had finally gotten up out of their armchairs. They wanted a little real action. They were the ones who complained most about the sun, and the primitive plumbing, and the fact that the only entertainment was a single radio tuned permanently to Libyan National Radio. This group was comprised mainly of Americans, former soldiers who wanted something to brag about later on. They'd probably get it, if they lived. Rosie knew it wasn't always the fanatics who died. It was just as often those who cared least. Too bad: they were good men, honest and loyal, at least in comparison to the rest. But they had survival on their minds before anything else. Rosie knew they'd be the first to lead a retreat if one were called. And maybe even if it weren't called.

Then there were the pros. Many of them were men not unlike the Black Berets. They tended to be French, seasoned by wars that were fought in an attempt to keep an empire from disintegrating. Mixed with the French were some South Africans and Rhodesians as well, white men who thought that human civilization was primarily a war between blacks and whites, with a few hours off now and again, for science, art, and religion. And Germans disgusted that their country's military had turned into simple brick-wall defense. These descendants of the fabled Prussian warriors couldn't stand that. The Germans made fine mercenaries.

The pros were dangerous. They were good men, most of them. Rosie respected them and knew he'd have to take them into careful account. He especially liked the French, who seemed to notice race and religion the least. They saw men and manhood first, and could gauge your skill to the ounce by the time they'd finished shaking your hand. They talked well, they ate well, they drank with gusto. They also shared their women with Rosie and he appreciated that. Too bad they were going to have to die.

Rosie didn't worry about it though, as he walked through the desert camp in his bright African clothes. He liked the outfit. The bold patterns and the earthy colors merged in a way that was pleasing to him. Still, he couldn't help but compare them with the black outfits that Billy Leaps had gotten for the team. This was a good masquerade, but Rosie—to tell the truth—would rather have been in the uniform of the Black Berets than wear anything else in the world. Heat or no heat. Bright patterns or not.

He was pondering that when the first explosion went off, a kind of throaty POW! It was intense enough that Rosie thought he could feel the earth move underneath the inch or two of sand that covered it. Everyone in the camp dived for cover, convinced they were under surprise attack. Dived for cover, as if their canvas tents could have provided shelter against anything more than an angry pigeon. The concussive slap of another explosion rent the air, and this time the earth did move, for sure.

The explosions reminded Rosie of the enormous bombs that the B-52s used to drop in 'Nam, bombs so big producing explosions so powerful that eardrums would burst if the bombardier was even a few feet off and allowed his load to drop too close to the Allied forces he was supposed to be protecting. Sometimes it was more than American eardrums that burst; sometimes it was whole American bodies. And sometimes they found pieces, but just as often they didn't. There was a third explosion, and then, in rapid succession, two more.

There was a rhythm to these blasts that Rosie recognized, the way you can recognize the characteristic way a friend blows an automobile horn.

While everyone else in the camp was hitting the dirt or hunting a weapon, Rosie just sauntered along the sandy, makeshift avenue. He wasn't worried. Applebaum was just showing off a little bit for his new commander, and Rosie wanted to go and say "hi."

Applebaum and Major Ascham were made for each other. Major Asshole had found somebody who'd listen to his stories. Applebaum would listen just so that he could fire back his own stories in return.

Over dinner, bullshit from one was shoveled on top of bullshit from the other. Rosie ate silently. He listened to Marty talk about Vietnam. Jesus Christ, you'd have thought the little guy had fought the war by himself. We would have won the thing in a year if there had been two Applebaums fighting instead of just one.

73

"Now Khe Sanh," Marty began, already dismissing Ascham's fabrications about the Rhodesian War of Independence, "Khe Sanh was hell. In four weeks we poured more metal on those gooks' heads than the whole goddamn Air Force dropped on Germany in the whole goddamn fucking World War II. It was great. I mean, it was wonderful. All fucking day long. The blood in your veins started pumping in the rhythm of the bombs. It was something else. Boom, boom, boom."

Rosie watched Marty. Little fella was just so excited about those goddamn bombs he probably had a hard-on. Nothing turned Marty on like bombs. His heart probably started to beat in time with the explosions.

The major wasn't impressed by bombs. "That was a technical war. You don't win technical wars anymore. Not against nontechnical people. That was the lesson of Vietnam. You Americans might as well have gone over and dropped computers on their heads for all the good your bombing did. You get a people like the Vietnamese—" Ascham suddenly glanced around the table, to make sure there weren't any Vietnamese actually sitting within earshot. There weren't, but he still went on a little more quietly, in case they were at the next table: "You take your basic Vietnamese, and he's backward, he's superstitious. He doesn't *understand* bombs or napalm. He thinks it's lightning from the sky. He thinks it's a bizarre weather pattern. Same thing with all these third-world people. What you've got to put before 'em is a little hand-to-hand combat. You have to stack one of your warriors against one of their warriors. That's what these people can understand. And that's why you've got to have people who can kill. People who can kill in a way that makes the enemy start to fear death. And what's more important, fear *you*. You Americans lost in Vietnam because the Vietnamese never got to see your faces. They saw the underbellies of the B-52s. That's what they saw, and that's why you lost."

Rosie was sick to his stomach of hearing why the United States lost the war in Vietnam. There were a hundred reasons, a thousand reasons, but only one reason that mattered. Because we didn't have to win it. That was clear in every decision that was ever made.

Ascham went on to count out a dozen ways to kill a man, most of them copped from the Nigerians. Rosie had heard them before. He was more interested in the bloodlust he saw in the Brit's eyes than in his stories. It looked real at the dinner table. But Rosie suspected that would drain right out those eyes when he was actually in the field, facing death on the other side of every piece of swelling ground, meeting death rising up out of every shadow, trying to shield himself from death that rained down out of every cloud.

It took a crazed man like Applebaum—or like himself, Rosie thought—to step into that same field and simply not care who walked away alive. That was their secret. That was their strength.

Rosie wasn't supposed to know Applebaum, so after the barracks dinner, he took up his promenade again. Up and down the regularly laid-out avenues, with the wind whipping his dashiki, and the sand blowing into his eyes. The only lights in the camp were those inside the tents so you could see the stars. That's how Rosie knew he was in the field. He could see millions of stars. In Newark, the streetlamps and the haze blocked them out. In the polluted cities of America, you saw only five of the millions you could see in the desert, in the jungle, in the mountain passes.

Up and down he went, lazily scouting out a piece of ass. At the same time, he was getting to know his enemy. He looked at everything. He listened carefully. You never knew what tiny piece of information held in the back of your head was going to make the difference between life and death. He looked closely at the faces that peered at him out of the tents. All those faces of people who were going to die. Every pair of eyes staring back at him innocent of the knowledge that the black man in the colorful dashiki would mark the boundary between their life . . . and their oblivion.

Of course that made the piece of ass a problem. Rosie didn't like the idea of screwing a woman he might have to kill. It took away his concentration. It might even take away his desire. After a slow stroll the length of the camp, Rosie decided that being alone was as good as not in this place.

11

Cowboy, Billy Leaps, and Tsali stood and looked at the electronic setup that was a part of the new house. It was contained in a small windowless room off the large common living room. The system was made up of four amber CRTs, three keyboards, and two disc drives on a long desk top built into the wall. Several file cabinets and other electronic workings in blue metal boxes were set neatly along another wall.

"Now, all you got to worry about is these two screens over here," said Cowboy to Tsali. "These are the ones that are gonna be important to you. They're both gonna be on twenty-four hours a day. Don't you worry about on switches and off switches 'cause there ain't any. You just leave them alone and you just worry about what they have to say to you."

Cowboy sat down at the wheeled chair that allowed him to scoot across the linoleum floor from one part of the setup to another. He went to the farther screen. It was the larger, nineteen inches diagonally. There were lines drawn on it, lines that replicated the outlines of Beeker's property. "See," said Cowboy, pointing at the screen, "here is the house, here is where we are." The form of Beeker's new house was traced in white lines on the amber screen. The tiny figure even showed the front and side doors of the building. All the other structures on the property were outlined in the same way, as well as the roads and fences. "So the whole farm is here," Cowboy concluded proudly. "The whole goddamn farm. Now, show me where our road meets the county road."

Tsali pointed to the junction unhesitatingly.

"Good," said Cowboy, then went on, "okay, so something man-sized walks onto the property, there are these sensors all along the perimeter. They pick up the motion and the body heat and they send the message to this here control center. It'll look like a little triangle, but it'll be flashing and probably moving. And there'll be a kind of beep-beep, like those arcade games we played the other day."

"What arcade games!" demanded Billy Leaps.

Cowboy sighed. Tsali bit his cheek to stop the smile of conspiracy that threatened his seriousness.

"You teaching Tsali to play fucking arcade games in some suburban shopping center?" The anger was clear in Billy Leaps's voice. "Bad enough you got him that goddamn television, now you're—"

"Beeker," Cowboy interrupted sharply, "I wanted the kid to see an electronic machine so he'd have a frame of reference, so we stopped and played a couple of games just so's he'd have a little experience. And test his reflexes. Kid's got great reflexes. Now can it, we don't have much more time and he's got to understand all this. And *this* piece of metal sure ain't no arcade machine."

Beeker growled, the same growl that came out of his throat every time one more of Cowboy and Tsali's secret adventures was uncovered. "Kid'll end up in Juvenile Hall."

"Not if he ever learns to use all this shit. Kid learns how to use this machine, he'll make enough money to make us look like beggars on the street." Cowboy slapped Tsali's back and smiled, then continued:

"So, anything man-sized comes in, you'll hear the little beep-beep. And here's what happens then." Cowbow pressed a button, and on the screen there appeared two concentric circles around the house, the inner circle in red, the outer in blue. "Two defense perimeters. If the triangle stays outside both of those, you're okay. If it breaches the outer one, you start to worry. Got it? If the movements are erratic, if they don't make any sense to you after you've watched for a while, you're okay too. Probably a deer. No way to keep the sensors from picking up anything as big as a man. So a deer could set 'em off. But a deer don't move like a man, or vice versa, we all know that. So you got it?"

Tsali nodded that he understood.

"Now, if this flashing triangle moves inside the defense

perimeter, that's an alert. The beep-beep gets louder and faster. That's when you go for your rifle. You've got a good five minutes from the final alert to get your rifle, get to the bunker.''

Tsali thought about the M-16 that Billy Leaps had finally showed him how to use. He nodded again. With a little sense of awe. It had been one thing to use a bow and arrow on a man, but after seeing what those tumbling 5.56-mm slugs could do to a target—any target—Tsali had every right to be awed by the machine's capability.

"No heroics," Cowboy warned in deadly seriousness. "You don't have to prove nothing to us. You got one job and that's to protect your ass and get to the bunker. That's why we built it. That's what it's for. No asshole stuff like Applebaum might pull. You just get to that bunker. You let them search this place if they want. There's nothing they'll find here except some nasty surprises. 'Cause when you get to the bunker, there's a switch for you to pull. It transfers everything out of here and puts it in there. All these screens go blank, and all the nasties turn on. And there's nothing else in this house. Nothing that's worth risking your hide for, anyway. Somebody wants to break up this hardware, fine, let 'em. We'll buy more. They want to burn down the house? We can build another. What we can't replace is you. You got that?''

Tsali nodded, though he knew he'd never follow Cowboy's orders in this. He'd never let another group of men torch the farm. Anyone who came near here while Tsali held the powerful M-16 would learn that this place was sacred. But he wasn't about to argue the issue anymore. He had tried once and Billy Leaps and Cowboy had refused to listen. It was enough that Tsali knew the truth himself.

"Course you're not gonna be sitting in this room the whole goddamn day—''

"Goddamn right about that!'' snarled Billy Leaps.

Cowboy paid no attention to the interruption. "—so if somebody gets inside the first defense perimeter there's gonna be a louder 'beep-beep' that'll sound in your room, in the hall outside all the bedrooms, at the front of the house, and in the barn. You should be able to hear it if you're within five hundred feet of the house.''

"And if you're any farther away from the house than that,''

said Billy Leaps, "you ought to have your gun with you anyway . . ."

"Goddamn it, Beak, let me get on with this! All right, kid, that alarm goes on, you follow your orders. But when you're sure it's all clear, you push this button here, see? And all the other alarms will stop. Now that's all you got to know about the security system. All it's designed to do, all it needs to do right now, is to give you warning to take cover. No one'll ever find that bunker now we got it camouflaged so well. You just go there, open that door, make love to your rifle, and wait till everything's over. You understand?"

Tsali did.

"All right, and tomorrow, I'm gonna show you how to communicate over this damn thing. How to send messages, and how to get messages. All right?"

Then Cowboy went through all the instructions again. He had Tsali play with the keyboard and act out all the various possibilities. How would he know if the perimeter was breached? How did he turn off the exterior alarms? Tsali breezed through the whole session. Beeker didn't know if he was pleased or alarmed by the boy's facility.

Billy Leaps was in a foul mood over the last evening meal the three of them shared. "Tsali needs to know if there's somebody out there. But he's never gonna understand all that fuckin' equipment."

Cowboy just smiled. Tsali got up to clear their dishes and bring coffee.

"It's too much for a kid who's led the kind of life he's led. For Christ's sake, he's a full-blooded Cherokee. He's not some computer whiz kid at Texas A&M. I want him to hunt and fish, I want him to do real stuff. I don't want him sitting in front of a TV screen all goddamn day."

Cowboy still said nothing, and Billy Leaps fell into silence too. Maybe he was wrong. Certainly he knew that electronics had a lot of importance on the battlefield. Anyone who had been in Vietnam and had watched the power and ability of the communications that could call forth an air strike or aim the guns of ships miles away from the target knew that. But Billy Leaps was trying to preserve the vision he had formed of himself and Tsali. In his mind, the two of them formed an inseparable bond, but the bond operated out of doors, in the forest, in the jungle, on the plains. They stalked deer for the table. They lived along a riverbank for a week at a time, with only their wits and their skill providing shelter and sustenance. Not father and son at matching computer consoles. Electronics in the form of arcade games and color televisions didn't have a place in Beeker's ideal vision.

But if Tsali wanted to learn about it, Beeker was thinking, electronics were the future and maybe he should let the boy go ahead. No, not maybe, Beeker *should* let him. He just didn't like the idea of Tsali's sitting in that windowless room, his face painted yellow by the glowing amber screen.

He looked at Tsali, pouring out the coffee, and realized that wasn't going to happen. Not to a sixteen-year-old who had killed three men with a bow and arrow. Not to a boy who had learned in a month to handle an M-16 better than most second-year recruits. Not to a kid who could live for a week out of doors without any special preparation.

Billy Leaps relaxed. He'd just have to trust Tsali. Then he realized, with a proud pang at his heart, that giving that trust to the boy was a pleasure in itself.

Tsali himself had every intention of becoming a warrior like this proud half-breed Cherokee—the man who would be his father. He felt the slightest bit guilty, however, that his loyalties were somewhat split. His pleasures were not wholly in the realm of hunting, fishing, and survival. He had loved the arcade games, and his excitement as the computer room was being put together was immense.

Especially because of the fourth console in the corner of the room, the one that Cowboy hadn't even turned on in Billy Leaps's presence. Because that was the simplest console, the one that played the arcade games that had hypnotized Tsali in the Shreveport mall. The cassettes for the games were kept in a paper bag at the back of the filing cabinet, and Cowboy warned him, "This is just for when we're not around. Don't you ever let Billy Leaps find out I've been corrupting you, boy. This is to pass the time when nobody's here. This is to make your reflexes quick.

That's all it is. Developing hand-eye coordination. *Star Wars* and *Zaxxon* are gonna make you a real killer with a M-16, kid."

They drank their coffee in silence. They could hear nothing but the hum of the refrigerator, and crickets chirping just outside the kitchen window. Cowboy still smiled at Beeker's objections. He knew that Beeker was remembering his own adolescence—when there was no adult male around to teach him to hunt, and shoot, and fish. He was trying to make up for his own deprivations by giving these things to Tsali. That was fine. Kid wanted those experiences. Beeker was the old man for Tsali. Cowboy wasn't going to interfere with that. But the kid had an unbounded curiosity about the world. Cowboy saw nothing wrong in letting him in on the secrets of electronics. There were games, sure. But there were also special training programs he had bought the boy, ones that would take him step by step through the mysteries of computers and their capabilities.

Beeker sometimes forgot how isolated the boy was, in his muteness. Beeker sometimes assumed that because he could understand the boy, everybody else could. That wasn't so. Computers might eventually provide Tsali with a kind of outlet for his hidden sociability that he had always been denied.

Kid'll grow up being an outdoorsman who can use a computer as well as he can fire a rifle, thought Cowboy. That's gonna be one hell of a kid. He's gonna make one hell of a soldier.

12

The training regimen didn't impress Rosie. Marksmanship was okay, not Black Berets standards though. Demolitions? Marty would have used up the camp's entire arsenal just for recreation if he had been allowed to go on. Strategy? Tactics? Major Ascham would have loved World War I.

These people were long on political rhetoric, short on scar tissue. It was clear they didn't respect their potential enemy, else they would have understood that training is what keeps a soldier alive in battle. Untrained is unskilled. Untrained usually ends up dead.

Rosie and Marty were both promoted quickly. Their skills were so great that they couldn't go unnoticed. Rosie was especially appreciated because he was black. The major might say, "We need to utilize your leadership potential," but that wasn't the whole story. They were going into some African country and it would look good if they had at least one black man in the command cadre. Rosie wondered what the target was. They still hadn't been told.

He didn't want to appear too curious, so he didn't ask. He played a little dumb—big black buck with a brain the size of a watermelon seed. He just bided his time. And he watched. He knew that these men and women would be his real enemy.

Harry came in a little after Applebaum. He had grown a beard, full and black, reaching high up on his cheeks. The beard only accentuated the sadness of Harry's eyes.

Now that three of them were together in the camp, Rosie worried. There was always a problem about covers like theirs. They could easily have given themselves away, done something that showed how close they had been. A glance that came too fast, a word or a name that betrayed too much common knowledge. Beeker had covered that a little bit—it was perfectly possible that Rosie and Harry and Marty had been in 'Nam together: bent a few elbows together in Da Nang bars, hunted whores in Saigon—whatever. So they could know each other and they'd all nod greetings. But they kept a careful distance from each other.

Rosie and Applebaum acknowledged Harry when he arrived, but they paid careful attention to the other officers. They wanted to make sure that Harry's cover was good.

An operation like this, one that had hired over three hundred mercenaries, couldn't have gone totally unnoticed. It would be unreasonable for Parkes, or anyone under him, to assume that it would. Major Ascham was suspicious of everyone, and had reason to be. An armed group of three hundred men and women loose in the world can light fires that four or five big-time nations would have trouble extinguishing. Look at Lebanon. The commander had to assume there were leaks. Leaks and spies.

As it turned out, Harry's cover was fine. Ascham was looking elsewhere.

It was too bad that Major Asshole's spy turned out to be Rosie's favorite Frenchman. Luc and Rosie had split a bottle of good Algerian wine the first night Rosie was in camp. They traded stories of whores in Marseilles and Saigon. They got along just fine.

Rosie never learned just how Ascham found out about Luc. The tall, skinny Frenchman was as innocent-looking as you could get. Turned out, though, he worked for French Intelligence. The French had to keep an eye on the other side of the Mediterranean—they had lots of investments in Africa, northern African in particular. So they wanted to know why there were three hundred armed men in a Libyan camp. Probably working the way the Black Berets had, they had sent Luc to infiltrate.

Major Asshole had paraded up the line of tents with four of his closest aides and had "arrested" Luc in the middle of the day. Ascham was a beefy man, too fat for real soldiering, so he had his goons do it.

While the four of them jumped Luc, Ascham tapped at the crease in his khaki uniform trousers with his swagger stick.

It took all four goons to get the Frenchman down. Two on each arm, even though he was skinny as a rail.

"Luc St. Jean?" Ascham spoke the name with a sneer. He came a step or two closer. "You aren't Luc St. Jean. Who are you?"

Luc took it like a pro, Rosie decided. Didn't argue, carry on, or plead. Didn't bluster. Whatever the game was, it was up, and Luc knew it. He lifted his head and spat a great gob of phlegm into Major Asshole's face, and lashed out a foot to crack against the Major's knee.

That hurt like hell, Rosie thought, and kept back a grin that wanted to come real bad.

Major Asshole jumped back in pain and humiliation. He lifted up his swagger stick and swung hard, slashing an ugly red welt across Luc's face. The four goons had hurriedly realigned themselves so that Luc couldn't retaliate again. Luc smiled, right at the Major. Rosie thought that was a class act, because the smile was contemptuous. Contempt for the Major, and for anything that Ascham could do to him. Contempt for the death that Luc must have known was not far off.

As Ascham wiped his face with a white kerchief he said, "Abdul Muhamed."

Rosie was suddenly sorry he had decided to watch all this. He should have melted away when he saw there was trouble coming. Goddamn.

Rosie stepped forward.

"We'll find out who you really are," said Ascham to the French prisoner.

Luc and Rosie looked at one another in a way . . . that was special.

In a camp of misfits and bantam cocks and bloodlusting harpies and Major Assholes, they were two pros. In that glance, lasting no more than a second or two, they acknowledged one another's true warrior status.

Luc was going to die. He knew that. He also knew that Rosie would be the one to kill him—that was why Ascham had called Rosie forward. Luc was asking Rosie for something important. Luc wanted to die with dignity.

*   *   *

They staked Luc out. Naked, his limbs were stretched tight by leather thongs that had been soaked in water. As the strips dried out and shrank in the hot sun, they cut painfully into his wrists and ankles. Rosie looked down at the spread-eagled form. Man was a *soldier*. You could see it in his body. He had looked skinny, but like Marty's, his skinniness was hard muscle. Everything else had burned off. His arms and legs looked like anatomy drawings.

The hot sun beat down on him. That part below Luc's waist was dead white, as if the Frenchman had never taken his pants off in the daytime before. His flesh was nearly hairless, just patches under his arms and around his cock. Thing was shriveled. The only fear that showed, Rosie thought with somber admiration.

Ascham was watching, making a big deal out of being a part of this. But like most real cowards, he made sure that he didn't see too clearly. He positioned himself behind Rosie, so that if things got too rough, he could use the black man to block his vision.

Rosie knelt down beside Luc, real close, and put a hand on the Frenchman's chest. He made believe he was checking out the bindings on his arms, but really he needed to speak to the Frenchman "You got something you can tell him?"

Luc looked at Rosie after he heard the whispered question. He didn't seem surprised that Rosie should speak to him. He knew that something special existed between the two of them.

Maybe Luc knew, or suspected, that Rosie was a spy and infiltrator, as well. But if he did, he also knew that there was no chance of reprieve. He did not in that glance say to Rosie, *Save me.* He knew Rosie wouldn't. It was the luck of the draw. In this draw Luc had been found out and would die. Rosie would be the instrument of his death, and would live. But Luc knew, and Rosie knew, that for the one who survived, there would be more draws down the line. And one day Rosie would lose the toss. And Rosie hoped there'd be someone there to make sure he'd die with dignity, too

"Yes," Luc answered. His lips didn't move. The word was barely a hiss.

"Can you come up with two things?"

"Yes."

Rosie patted Luc's chest once and stood up again. "So what you want to know, Major?"

Ascham looked down at the stretched figure. "I want to know his real name."

Rosie took a pair of pliers, hard-steel hot from the sun. He bent over and caught one of Luc's flat tits in between the corrugated teeth of the tool. He pulled straight up with a jerk. Luc screamed.

He pulled harder on the handle of the pliers. And twisted. It looked worse than it was. Especially on a man like Luc, who didn't have any flesh to spare.

Rosie had Luc's nipple up a good six inches in the air. He was squeezing blood out of it. The unnatural cone of skin was ripping all around.

It was probably no more painful, in reality, than getting a few fingers lopped off. One by one.

Rosie twisted the pliers, crushing the nipple.

The nerves would have been severed by now. Luc probably couldn't feel it at all.

Rosie sneaked a glance at Ascham.

The major was pale. Sweat beaded on his forehead.

"I'll tell!" Luc screamed.

Rosie tore the nipple loose, and dropped it in the sand.

The skin of Luc's breast, pulled out of shape, fell back to his chest. The wound oozed blood.

Luc gave Major Asshole another one of those improbable French names. It must have been correct, because Major Asshole let it go.

"I want him to die slowly. Horribly," said Ascham in a choked voice. He was staring at the little bloody crown of nipple, still visible in the sand at his feet.

Rosie was thrown off. "No more questions?"

"We know all about him now," said Major Asshole, getting back his composure. "That's who we thought he was. Now we're certain. A French operative who worked against Qadhafi a few years back. He had nerve to come back to Libya. Real nerve. If they had found him"— Major Asshole smiled a cruel smile— "but now I've found him."

86

"Leave him here," suggested Rosie. "Let the sun get him. And thirst." *And I'll come back in the evening.*

"No," said Ascham. "Torture. I want him to die now and painfully. Just in case there are any other infiltrators here. I want them to know what we'll do when we find them out. I want a little discouragement." Rosie had heard that tone of voice in men before. This man wanted to watch. Wanted to see a better man die badly. Rosie had methods, of course he had methods, but he wasn't about to use them on Luc. He was trying to think of a way out of this.

Luc was looking right at Rosie. Here and there his body twitched, uncontrollably. But he had that courage still on his face. He was asking Rosie not for mercy, but for dignity. He didn't want to die a blubbering idiot. But how could Rosie honor that basic request and still keep Major Asshole satisfied?

Rosie once again knelt at Luc's side. Taking the pliers once more, he tore off the Frenchman's remaining nipple. Luc screamed, and Rosie, who was a judge of such things, could tell by its intensity and pitch just how much pain the man really was suffering. Luc was weakening. The sun did that.

"Slower," said Ascham. "I want him to suffer slowly."

"I'm just starting," said Rosie. He took a knife out of his belt, and with just a small amount of pressure ran the blade from Luc's neck, down his chest and belly, and into his pubic hair. This left a long red line of welling blood, and it looked bad, especially with the lacerated flesh of Luc's tits.

But to a man suffering in the African sun, with shrinking leather straps holding him down, it was more like a tickle than a cut.

Luc played along. He squirmed against his leather bondage.

Looked pretty good, Rosie judged, so he continued.

"Blood," said Major Asshole huskily.

Good, thought Rosie, *that was the way.*

He drew parallel lines across the Frenchman's belly. The skin seemed to shrink back from the cuts. Blood seeped upward, soaking the skin. It dripped off into the sand.

One of the goons spoke to the Major, and Rosie took the opportunity of that covering voice to say to Luc, very quietly, "It'll be quick."

Luc's eyes closed once, in strange gratitude. Then his body began to shake again.

Blood? You want blood, Major Asshole? You got blood, Rosie thought. His knife was sharp. Scalpel sharp. He kept it that way. He made lacerations in Luc's sinewy thighs. He cut the tendons around Luc's knees.

"See," said Rosie, grinning up at Ascham. "Fucker can't run away now."

Major Asshole and his goons laughed.

And while they were laughing, Rosie drew the knife once more straight up from Luc's belly to his neck. And pressed the tip into the Frenchman's jugular. It wasn't hard to find. Rosie could see it, pumping blood into Luc's brain. The incision was just a flick of Rosie's wrist. It might have been a slip, but it wasn't.

A fountain of Luc's blood rose in pulsing rhythms up into the air. It splashed down in decreasing waves across his already reddened body. Aloud, Rosie counted the pulses with which Luc's heart poured out his blood and his life upon the sand.

"One. Two. Three. Four. Five."

The sixth was barely detectable.

There was no seventh.

Luc didn't scream. But there was knowledge and gratitude in his eyes, until his eyes glazed over. And there was a smile on his lips for Rosie, until his mouth fell slack in death.

Rosie stood. Luc was a warrior. An honorable man who had fallen into a trap, who had refused to act like a snared animal. No panic, no regrets, no begging. The kind of man Rosie could respect. It was too bad he had to go.

But Luc's death would make the deaths to follow just that much easier.

13

They slept. All three of them in their own rooms, small concrete rectangles that held a bureau and a plain single bed. All the privacy a man needed. It was like the barracks Cowboy and Beeker had grown used to, and more than the kid had ever had. They each had dreams. Pleasant dreams. The security of the house. The sense of purpose they all felt. After the years they had wandered through life, undirected, unattached, they had a life worth living now. Their dreams were of fine women and long fishing trips, good food and high-powered planes . . .

Beep-beep. Beep-beep.

The alarm.

Cowboy shot up, the way a combat flyer always does. The alert was on. The need to be ever ready. For a moment he wondered why he didn't have on his flight suit, the way he always did in 'Nam. The suit that he wore sleeping when he was on call, always prepared to take up whatever machine they had assigned him that week to strike hard and fast at the enemy. Where was his suit?

Beep-beep. Beep-beep.

The electronic noise echoed in the hall, out of doors. The alarm. Fucking deer, Beeker thought when he heard it. Goddamn thing's going to wake up Tsali every night when a goddamned deer walks into the perimeter. Kid'll be a nervous case. In his blurred sleep, his thoughts heavily influenced by the distrust he had for the machines, Beeker thought he should pull the plug so they could all get a good . . .

"Don't turn on the lights. Leave your lights off!" Cowboy's voice showed the absolute trust he had in the machine, trust as intense as Beeker's doubt. He raced down the corridor in his

89

underwear, stopping only to punch the alarm-off button by the door of Tsali's room. He raced into the computer room.

Cowboy studied the screen with the farm's map on it intently. Beeker had followed him in and was leaning over his shoulder trying to decipher the messages of intrusion that the sophisticated machinery showed him. Tsali hung back at the doorway, watching the screen's light reflect off the bodies of the two muscular men clad only in their Jockey shorts. Cowboy's face showed he was wide awake and totally alert. "Kid's got time to see this. Come here, Tsali." He waved the boy in.

Tsali walked up to the screen and followed Cowboy's finger as it traced the progress of two pairs of flashing triangles on the glass. The motion was slow but steady, and it was obvious the intruders were headed directly for the house.

"Ever seen goddamn deer pair off and advance like that?" Cowboy asked Beeker sarcastically.

"You think they heard the alarm?" Beeker asked.

"Don't think so," said Cowboy. "I got it off quick. They aren't slowing down."

Beeker and Cowboy broke away from the screen. Cowboy didn't need orders, and Beeker didn't need conversation. They each went to the storage room where the arms were kept. Cowboy grabbed his M-16. "Want Applebaum's M-60?" he asked Beeker.

"I don't need anything but my own rifle," Billy Leaps replied. He reached past Cowboy and took it from its perch. The two men went through the procedure of checking the weapons, the ammunition, grabbing a butt pack full of clips. They did it without thought. They had done it so often, for so many years, there was nothing but utter and effortless accuracy in their efforts. The rifles were ready. They always were.

Beeker would have gone directly outside, but Cowboy motioned him toward the computer room once more. He checked the screen again as he stepped into a dark sweatsuit. The four triangles had shifted their positions.

"These two are coming head on," said Cowboy, pointing. "These two have split up. They're coming for the front of the house too, but from different angles. So one from each side, and two exactly frontal."

They unbolted the front door, eased outside, and took up their positions at the front of the house. No time for camouflage. No time for uniforms. The night air chilled Beeker's nearly naked skin. They hid behind the enormous evergreens that had been planted all around the house, not for aesthetic reasons, but for a purpose just such as this. For cover in case of attack. And to make the house seem a little less of a fortress than it actually was.

They waited. Gravel cut into Beeker's bare feet. He chose not to notice. In the past he had ignored so many different discomforts while waiting in ambush that this was minor beyond thought. His ears were alert. The sounds of the forest night around the camp came to him clearly. Nesting birds suddenly setting up a sleepy squabble. A cricket's insistent song, slowed by the night air. The wind now and then through the top of the loblolly pines. And a mechanical click behind him.

Beeker didn't tense at all. It was Tsali preparing his own rifle.

While he tried to lecture himself—*should have told him to stay in his room . . . or go to the bunker*—Beeker was proud the boy had automatically assumed his own defensive position, had gotten himself ready to help him and Cowboy defend the house.

There was a noise to the right. A man's foot on a twig. But the three defenders held. They knew there were four men coming. They would have to wait till all four were in the clearing before the house. All four of the invaders had to be gotten in this counterambush. Shoot just one and the other three are going to be aware of how much firepower you have, where you are, what you have to fight with.

The moon, no more than a sliver, was high in a black sky. It cast a dim pallor over the landscape, but it was enough for Beeker's night-accustomed eyes to see by.

He could see the man on his right now. He was standing very still beside the thick trunk of an oak—one of the trees that Tsali had used for target practice. He must be waiting for the others. Beeker's eyes kept darting, first making sure that the one invader wasn't moving closer, then trying to see where the others were.

The lawn all around the house had been made wide and deep. There was no way of approaching the building without stepping into the unprotected space. If anyone was fool enough . . .

Someone was. The second man, on the frontal pair. *Idiot,* thought Billy Leaps. *You'll die for that.*

These two were his. The one he had spotted first and the one in front. He trusted Cowboy to know that these were now the two men Beeker would take out. Now he just needed the signal that the flyer had the other two in his own sites.

Beeker was cold. He felt like a primitive warrior out there in the night with almost nothing on. He could smell himself. No clothes, no thick uniform for the perspiration to soak through. Just a man's smell, the feel of his rifle against his naked shoulder, his armor nothing but his skill.

Crack. Cowboy's M-16 opened fire on Beeker's left. Without any conscious thought on his part, Beeker's weapon—that length of metal, plastic, and death that had become an extension of his own flesh—Beeker's '16 opened up, sending the rounds of burning metal through the air. Quick death, flying toward the intruders who dared to come here, to Beeker's farm, the Black Berets' fortress.

He had known just how he'd do it. Never even thought about it, he had just known. With surprise all on his side, and with all the time he had needed to gauge the distance of his foes, Beeker first took out the one on his right. A volley immediately followed Cowboy's single shot, cutting through the branches of the oak the man thought was shielding him. He had time to give one hoarse cry, and then death cut short even that one brief protest.

Then that strange thing happened that always happens in these very quick, very sudden skirmishes and ambushes. Time changed, the very nature of it. It became divided into fractions of itself. It was as if each tenth of a second lasted a full minute, and gave Beeker time to figure out exactly what was happening. First he had heard Cowboy's shot, and he assumed one man down. Then he had fired off his own volley. A second man down. And during this man's final groan, he heard a third shot—but it wasn't Cowboy's M-16 that fired. It was Tsali's. *Good,* thought Beeker. It never occurred to Billy Leaps to doubt that Tsali had taken out the third man.

Billy Leaps thought, *I couldn't be here the first time. I'm glad I'm here now.*

The first time, that is, that Tsali had killed a man.

92

The fourth man, with a look of fear on his face illumined by the sliver of moon, raised his rifle. Then the look of fear was gone—because so was the face that had borne it. The second burst from Beeker's rifle had been quick and accurate. The rifle kept on rising in the headless man's arms. There was no brain to tell the muscles to stop.

Silence again. Silence after death. A moment of absolute stillness on the farm.

Then the crickets resumed their chirping. A gust of wind blew through the loblollies. A bat flapped its leathery black wings near the chimney of the house.

"That's it," said Cowboy, his pale white face reflecting the moonlight eerily. "Got 'em."

"Tsali," said Billy Leaps quietly, "which one was yours?"

The boy pointed ahead. A man's corpse lay within a few yards of the man whose head Billy Leaps had blown off.

"Stand guard," said Billy Leaps. He knew all four men were dead. There was no question in his mind that the thing had been done right. It felt right. But he always took care, and he also wanted to teach the boy to take care. So he kept Tsali on guard for them, against the four dead men.

Because, sometimes, dead men rose up on the elbows and, with the last ounce of their treasured strength, put a bullet in your brain.

Billy Leaps and Cowboy went to the left with their own rifles ready. Cowboy's shot had been clean and precise, right through the neck.

Beeker shook his head. "Cowboy, you always go for the neck. One of these days you're gonna miss, and you're gonna get the booby prize. Some fucker is gonna want shoot back."

Cowboy grinned. "Never happened yet, Beeker."

They dragged the corpse to the front of the house, and laid him at Tsali's feet. They went to the corpse of the man that the boy had killed, and dragged him over too.

Beeker silently pointed out to Tsali the two wounds in the man's body, one in the chest, the other in the abdomen. "Either one would have killed him," said Billy Leaps, "but this one"—he pointed to the chest—"this one also kept him from firing back."

"Good work, kid," said Cowboy, adding what Billy Leaps would not.

Then they collected the other two. Cowboy made Beeker take the headless one. "I don't mind dead bodies," he explained. "It's parts I can't stand. So if you're gonna be so goddamn messy, you can goddamn well clean it up yourself."

"Turn on the lights, Tsali," said Billy Leaps. The boy opened the front door, reached inside, and flicked on the lights over the small porch. The four corpses at the foot of the front steps were suddenly bathed in a harsh, heavily shadowing spotlight. The flesh seemed livid, the blood looked thick and black.

Cowboy and Beeker methodically went through the clothing of the corpses for identification. To their amazement, they found it.

"This has got to be fake," Cowboy said as he held up a Maryland driver's license he had discovered in one man's wallet. There were even credit cards, a personal note with a telephone number on it, all the things a man might carry around with him if he were going out for a beer—but not if he planned to assault an armed camp.

Beeker had found similar identifications on the other two men. Two more Maryland licenses, one from Virginia. Pictures of girl friends or wives, an identity card from a security outfit, receipt for payment of union dues. He stood up, frowned at the dead men, and shook his head.

"These aren't fakes," he said. "May not be their real names, but they're the ones they really use."

"What you mean?" Cowboy asked.

Beeker stooped and shoved all the cards into the pocket of the corpse nearest him. "Let's bury them. Quick."

"Kid's going to think he's growing up in a goddamn cemetery," said Cowboy, as he and Beeker, now dressed, retrieved the backhoe from the new barn.

"He's all right," said Beeker. "But let's leave him alone for a few minutes."

They attached the corpses to the backhoe, and dragged them out into the fields where next spring Beeker expected to plant a good-sized plot of corn. Next year they'd be able to find the spot again easily. The corn would be higher there, and greener.

The backhoe made quick work covering over the four corpses. Cowboy would have buried the rifles with them, but Billy Leaps was against burying anything that wouldn't rot and return to the earth. The rifles went into the gun room. The work these men had planned would ensure that there were no records of these guns . . . anywhere.

When the men were done they went back into the house. It was nearly dawn. Tsali had made coffee. It was waiting. Cowboy said nothing. Times like this you didn't talk to Billy Leaps till he decided he wanted conversation. Cowboy knew that. He brought a bottle of brandy over to the table and poured himself a shot. Beeker waved away the flyer's offer for one himself.

He sipped his coffee, looking at Tsali so hard the kid began wondering if Billy Leaps was going to blame *him* for the attack. Or admonish him for the killing.

"Sit down, son."

Cowboy suddenly relaxed. Billy Leaps had spoken at last, and his tone was soothing.

The words had the opposite effect on Tsali. They made him more nervous and excited than before. Billy Leaps had never called him *son* before.

"They were after you, Tsali. They wanted to get you. If they had thought there were three of us here, they would never have come at the house like that."

"What makes you so sure?" Cowboy demanded. While Beeker's first logic was sound enough, Cowboy wasn't positive. You never really found out for sure what dead men had been thinking.

"It's Parkes," said Billy Leaps. "I know it's Parkes. Look, Cowboy, he saw you take off the other night. Probably had somebody watching the place, waiting—this was before we had the surveillance system going, remember? Somebody saw the men get in your plane and fly away—and they thought we were all gone. And that the boy was here alone."

"But nobody knows about the boy," Cowboy argued.

"Dozens of people know about the boy," said Beeker, studying the coffee cup in front of him. "Dozens. You trying to tell me that all the guys who built this place didn't see the way I treat the kid? The way we all treat him? And don't people see us when we go into town, buy him shit? Take him to the goddamn video

95

arcade in the goddamn mall? You think people don't see . . ."
Beeker stopped for a moment. His motion of sipping the coffee
wasn't very convincing, but he needed it to continue.

". . . you think people don't see how a father looks at his son,
how a father's friends look at his son?"

Beeker didn't look at either Cowboy or Tsali as he spoke these
words.

They were silent for a few moments.

At last Beeker looked up, and when he did, he gaze was on
Tsali. "Tsali, Parkes wanted to get you to hurt me. I don't know
if he was going to kidnap you, or just planned to kill you and
burn this place down again. It doesn't matter. He was going to
hurt all of us. So you have to be careful, very careful. You have
to be on alert as though you, yourself, were in the field. Because
that's exactly where you are now. You have food. You have
everything here you need. Don't ever, *ever* leave this farm when
we're not here. And don't ever turn off that fucking machine in
there."

Then he turned to Cowboy. "We gotta get him. We gotta get
Parkes and take him out. A few weeks ago he sent in three men.
Tonight he sent in four. And he's not the kind who's gonna stop.
He's gonna keep hiring these people, and one day he's gonna
find some lucky ones who get through our defenses. So that just
means we gotta get him. As long as Parkes is alive, Tsali's in
danger. And I'm not gonna have my boy grow up like that."

"We're gonna get him," said Cowboy soothingly. But the
words were also a vow. You could tell. He turned and looked at
the boy. "We're gonna take him out."

14

Major Ascham had called them all together into the mess tent, the largest of the camp's buildings, but still a pretty rickety structure. The tables had been folded up, and the chairs rearranged auditorium style. Rosie took a place on the side, and watched everything like a good little soldier. The motley crew gathered. If this had been the United Nations, there might have been a chance for peace in the world. Where else would you find black men who fought in Biafra sitting down with whites who had done battle in Rhodesia? Or Turks who had invaded Greece rubbing elbows with Cypriots who had cut their teeth in their own nasty civil war?

You had Irish talking to English Tommies. Frenchmen shared their meals with Algerians. You name the conflict, any one of the wars that had kept the world's blood running from open sores, and both sides were represented here.

This was an army of soldiers without a cause. A collection of men and women instructed in the use of a hundred weapons, equipped to fight in a dozen climates, trained to kill without remorse or mercy. And beyond survival, the paymaster was the only thing they cared about.

"We have a training mission to perform," Major Ascham announced to his assembled troops. "You all appreciate the obvious fact that the People's Government of Libya has generously allowed our Liberation Army to train here unmolested. While they—as a member of the world community—could never publicly acknowledge this kindness to us, they have asked that we perform a small task in repayment of their . . . hospitality."

A murmur of approval swept through the ranks. *Christ*, thought Rosie, *they're fucking sixth graders, listening to the principal.*

Rosie looked across the way and caught Harry's eye. The two Black Berets held that glance perhaps a second or two too long. But in the midst of all this dangerous idiocy, Rosie and Harry needed that extra second or two of sane companionship. Rosie broke away and searched for Applebaum. He found the little guy way to the right, his once pale skin ablaze with red from the bruising Saharan sun.

Oh hell, Marty.

Applebaum was a danger when he was let loose this way. He might lose his touch with reality. Forget he was part of the team. Get swept up with the rest of these cracked skulls. Rosie saw that he would have to talk to Marty. The little man was watching Ascham with the fervor of a true believer.

"There is a small independent nation, just to the southwest of here." Ascham was pointing to a large map of North Africa now, his stick indicating the tiny capital of a backward black African nation. "This country—Bashi—has, of late, proved itself quite an annoyance to our Libyan hosts.

"Now as you may or may not know, the boundary between Libya and Bashi is under dispute. It always has been, but of late border skirmishes have increased in violence and intensity. They are an annoyance to Colonel Qadhafi. They distract him from larger concerns." Here Major Ascham smiled. He let his troops decide for themselves what Colonel Qadhafi's greater concerns might be.

"It is also the case, I'm sorry to say, that the Libyans have not always come out on top in these skirmishes. And one of the reasons for the kingdom of Bashi's success in this border conflict has been the presence of a hospital—"

A hospital, thought Rosie. *Goddamn. What the fuck next?*

"—approximately *here.*" Ascham pointed at the map. "The hospital was founded in the middle of the last century by an order of Ursuline nuns, but we have evidence now that this convent-hospital operates both as an ammunition dump and training facility for Bashi soldiers engaged in the border conflict. Without this hospital—this training camp and arms dump"—the Major quickly corrected himself—"there is no doubt that the Libyans would have no difficulty in crushing the Bashi, and reestablishing their rightful borders."

A slight murmur of approval went through the assembly. What Major Asshole said apparently made sense to the greatest number.

Ascham stood at his own kind of attention, legs wide spread, the swagger stick held at its extremities by both hands. "Your task—a training mission for our purposes, and a way to thank our Libyan hosts at the same time—is to eliminate this false and vexatious institution. There will, of course, be a combat bonus for all of you."

Once more Rosie exchanged a glance with Harry. They couldn't help it.

Rosie caught up with Applebaum after dinner that night. The little blond man was having great fun in Libya. For one thing, the dry desert air cleared up his sinuses. He didn't wheeze anymore. Besides, Marty had himself a ball with all the other crazy people. That was part of Rosie's problem with him. You put a crazy man in a psych ward with two hundred other crazy people and he forgets he's off. He forgets that sane people act different, real different.

Rosie took Marty for a walk. For a while he humored him, letting Marty go on and on about the people he'd met, the stories he'd heard, and the stories he'd told himself.

"You sleeping with your M-16?" Rosie asked.

"Naw." Marty's chest pushed out. It was funny to see the little five-seven man being cocky that way next to Roosevelt Boone, who stood six foot of heavy muscle in his stockinged feet. "Naw, not the M-16. I sleep with my M-60, my baby." The enormous machine gun was probably as big as Marty, and how he was able to carry it around all by himself was a daily miracle in Rosie's eyes. "All the guys think it's real awesome I sleep with it."

"I think you're just being your usual asshole self," Rosie said calmly.

Marty stiffened with anger and injured pride. "These people think *I'm* awesome."

Rosie sighed. "Marty, they're Parkes's people. They are the enemy, and one of these days, remember, you and me are gonna have to off 'em. What you paying attention to them for?"

Applebaum stopped suddenly, and looked at Rosie wide-eyed.

Not a minute too soon, thought Rosie.

"What's our mission?" Rosie asked.

"To get Parkes."

Rosie nodded. "And what about his people? What about Major Asshole?"

"He gets it too," said Marty, his eyes tightening as he looked around him.

"And what about these guys who think you're so awesome?"

"Them too," said Applebaum, a little hesitantly.

"Them too," confirmed Rosie. "Why them too?"

" 'Cause they're assholes, they're Parkes's assholes."

"And because if we don't get them, they're gonna get us. Got it now?"

"Yeah," said Marty. "Yeah, I got it. We're gonna give it to 'em. Every one of the fuckers. Every one. I can't wait, Rosie. I just can't wait. I'll show 'em what awesome really is."

"Fine. Fine. You go on back now. I'll wait here and follow in a couple of minutes. Don't want us seen together too much, Marty. Be careful. Be awesome all you want. But be careful, too. 'Cause we got to make sure we get everybody. You got it all now? You got it straight? You know you're not supposed to listen to these assholes, 'cause all these assholes are gonna die—you know that, don't you?"

Marty nodded understanding to everything, and then suddenly he was gone. Disappeared into the desert night.

Rosie leaned against the crumbling wall. The surface was powdery and smelled of the sun. Just a little cheerleading, that's all it was. Just coming across a blind man walking down the sidewalk, and turning him a little, so he didn't walk out in the street in front of a truck. That's all. In the huddle together, and pointing out which was the right goal post, just so nobody'd forget and give the score to the wrong team.

Major Ascham stood by the waiting helicopters. Their markings had been recently painted over. Rosie wondered where they came from. Not that it mattered. You could buy just about any armaments you wanted nowadays. In a couple more years you'd probably be able to procure a little atomic bomb on the open market.

With Applebaum at the head of the line. What the hell were they going to do with Marty then? Rosie could see Applebaum cuddling up every night with his arms around a tactical nuclear missile.

But Marty wasn't the problem right now. He had remembered his lesson from the other night. He was standing near Rosie now, and close behind him was Harry. The Greek's expression seemed even sadder than usual. He hated Libya as much as Applebaum loved it.

The helicopter engines were revving up. The multinational force that Parkes had assembled was a little United Nations of death. That's what was right here in the middle of the sun-bleached African desert.

Marty was standing, draped with belts of ammo and his M-60—how *did* that little man carry the weight? Harry had one too, but it made sense for the Greek. For Harry's bulk, the M-60 was almost in scale. Rosie had only his M-16. That and a whole set of LAWs. Rosie had known just what to do when he saw those in the camp stockpile. The deadly missiles, originally designed as an antitank weapon, were just the thing. If modern warfare had to come up with a disposable weapon, this was it. Pop the top. Pull the tube. Point and shoot. One missile each, one explosive charge. What would they think of next? Rosie didn't know, but he did know it was just what he wanted for this mission.

The strike force was composed of fifty of the three hundred. This was to be their training mission. The one where they got their blood baptism. It was an affecting ceremony, as long as you weren't the one bleeding.

Ascham had chosen the group carefully—this was a reward for some, a test for others. Rosie knew Major Asshole would keep careful track of it all. If the raid on the hospital was a test of their skill, so too was their willingness to go a test of their commitment.

So these were the first fifty. The fifty who were going to be the vanguard of any force. Once these were taken out, the rest of Parkes's crew looked pretty puny. These fifty had given the whole group a backbone, and without them, the others wouldn't be worth shit. Rosie had made sure that he, Harry, and Marty were right there in front.

Now they were going.

At a signal from Ascham, the group fell into four squads, and began to climb aboard the choppers. As planned, Marty ran up to Major Asshole. "Which one's first? I want to be on the first one!"

Marty was probably the only thirty-five-year-old man on earth who could have said something like that and made it sound like honest enthusiasm.

Ascham smiled. He'd taken a shine to Marty. *Raise a hand of greeting to the departing troops, Major,* thought Rosie. *I who am going to survive this fucking war salute you, who are about to die.* The high whine of the turbines broke into his reverie and he and Harry climbed into the lead chopper.

15

Cowboy revved up the engines of the Beechcraft. The twin-engined plane powered noisily. Then, as though it were a bronc let loose from a corral, it jumped forward, hurtling itself and its pilot down the disguised runway. He got takeoff speed easily. As soon as they broke free, Cowboy flipped a button on his console to up the landing gear.

As he soared into the sky Cowboy looked back and saw the figures of Tsali and Billy Leaps Beeker standing in the front yard of the new house. The boy was waving. Even though he knew Tsali couldn't see him, Cowboy lifted his own hand. *Good kid. Fuckin' great pair, him and Billy Leaps.*

Cowboy felt a sympathetic pang for his friend Billy Leaps. Must be shit to get hold of a kid like that and find him endangered by the very relationship that seemed like such a salvation for both of them. Man wandering the earth without a child. Boy wandering without a father. They find one another and some asshole like Parkes plans to step in and end it all.

The Beechcraft headed south, for Mexico City. Cowboy had filed all the necessary legal documents and his flight plans. The trip looked routine and was handled quietly. But Parkes would know about it if he had someone planted at the small Shreveport airport. Billy Leaps hadn't wanted to make it too difficult for Parkes to find Cowboy.

But they didn't know what kind of real organization Parkes had. How wide was his net? And how far and how quickly could it be cast? How much manpower did he have to direct against them? It was possible that those three intruders who had come to burn the farm were the whole of Parkes's army. It was more likely that they were an insignificant percentage of what Parkes could muster. How could they know? There were only six persons on earth who they were certain did not belong to Parkes: the five of them, and Tsali. Anybody else—anybody else at all—might easily be in Parkes's employ. They made guesses, and they tried to reason it out, but it was the kind of speculation that led to paranoia, so Billy Leaps had stopped it. "Take what comes," he advised. "Just always be ready."

After Applebaum, Rosie, and Harry had gone, Beeker waited a couple of days to make sure no discouraging messages were sent back, then said to Cowboy, "I'm sending you out on point."

Cowboy didn't understand at first. In the field in 'Nam, you had to have someone at point, one man leading the forces, leaving himself vulnerable to the first attack. It was the kind of thing only a fool like Applebaum volunteered for. It was the kind of thing that a member of the team accepted when it came his turn. This trip to Mexico City was Cowboy's—it was his time to be at point.

"He's out there. Somewhere," said Beeker, and he didn't need to say aloud that he was referring to Parkes.

"And I'm gonna draw his fire," said Cowboy.

Cowboy didn't fear the assignment, but even if he had, he would never have refused it. He had just become the most vulnerable member of the team. It would be his duty to test the strength of the enemy, to find out just what kind of forces the Black Berets would be pitted against.

But the danger of the mission wasn't foremost in Cowboy's mind, not once he had crossed into Mexican airspace. Cowboy never could think just about combat when he was in Latin America. Too many memories—wonderful memories—crowded in on him. He let the plane go its course and he thought about his Spanish women. He liked their sun-darkened skin. He liked the particular way they tasted, so different from American women, from African women, from Chinese women, from . . .

It happened to him every time he crossed the Rio Grande. He realized he'd be flying over Guadalajara. What was her name? Rosa? He might even have married her. Cowboy had married a number of Latin American ladies. Cowboy loved getting married: the big ceremonies, the wonderful honeymoons, the adoring wives—they all had a special place in his heart.

Rosa in Guadalajara. Now he remembered. It had been one of the best weddings. A band. A hacienda in the mountains for their wedding night. A full week—maybe even ten days—of wedded bliss.

That was the problem, of course. The bliss never lasted longer than that. And neither did Cowboy. He always told himself that he'd come back to Rosa—or to whomever—and he meant it. But before he could get back to Rosa—or to whomever—there was another bride, and another band, and another honeymoon.

Cowboy had a mental list of cities that he ought not to return to. Latin daddies got upset when their daughters were left behind. It was hard to explain to them that it was better this way. So much better. You go in, play the romance, make the proposal, have the big party, luxuriate in the honeymoon—and then you leave. Before she gets fat and you get mean.

Tsali's entry into their lives had changed more than one perception. Cowboy had never really thought about it before. What if he had a kid of his own? No reason one or more of those weeks of wedded bliss shouldn't have produced a little mixed-breed cowboy. Or a little cowgirl with brown skin and blue eyes. Jesus, what a heavy thought. Bad enough that Cowboy had had to cut down on the dope and the coke when they went into the field. These past few months were the only period in years that Cowboy had operated with total lucidity. If he ever had before. It had been strange to stop all that stuff at once. What if he had a kid somewhere? What if this kid needed a father the way Tsali did? Jesus, another heavy thought.

Cowboy was sobered. He actually began to hope that he didn't find anybody to marry in Mexico City. Despite the possible danger, he had been happy to get this assignment—days by himself in the capital city, with all the time in the world to find a new lady. But fuck it, what if it meant a kid somewhere down the line? A kid who would grow up without a father. Cowboy was actually shuddering as he brought the Beechcraft down onto the airport runway. Jesus, talk about heavy . . .

Cowboy was on point.

He walked through Mexico City as an open target. He cradled the Browning Hi-Power he had gotten hold of first thing. It rested in a shoulder holster now. His only protection. Cowboy was a pilot, he was supposed to be in the air, flying. But the team needed someone to stand out in the open and draw fire. If there was fire to draw.

Cowboy walked the boulevards of Mexico City, alert, ready, watching all the time he was trying desperately to appear nonchalant. He sat in sidewalk cafes. He danced at big discos with women who were ostentatiously part of the jet set. He ate lunch at the best-known tourist places. He made himself as obvious as any man could be in a city with a population of over fifteen million.

After a few days of this incessant round of public display, Cowboy felt sure that of those fifteen million people there wasn't one man, woman, child, or babe at the breast who hadn't seen him.

He played the part of just another Texas tourist so well there were moments he forgot he was a target. Waiting for someone to put a bullet between his eyes, or a knife in his ribs, in exchange for an envelope full of American dollars, handed over by Parkes himself.

He met a woman. Nice woman. Big breasts, firm buttocks. She had been dancing at one of those glittering discos that Cowboy went to. She liked the dark glasses he wore even at night, even indoors in the uncertain flickering illumination. She liked his slim hips, his liquid movements. She liked the way he kissed. Cowboy knew you had to start easy when you kissed a lady, make her think you're going to treat her delicately. Then, when you've proved to her that you're trustworthy, you can give her what she really wants. That was Cowboy's secret. Start with what women think they want. Then act on what you know they want.

Worked like a charm. She was from Acapulco. She had a husband, so they couldn't get married. Cowboy liked that part.

She made Cowboy's job easier. Made him look all the more exposed to anyone who might be stalking him. He courted her, cooed over her. At those sidewalk cafes, he treated her like she was the Madonna, and he needed to get into heaven. He picked roses for her at the street-corner stands, and never once allowed her to pay for the smallest purchase. He gave every appearance of being totally absorbed by her.

Eight days passed this way. No one made an attempt on his life. No one even attempted to lift his wallet. Billy Leaps called early one morning, and to his single question, "Anything?" Cowboy replied, "Nothing."

"Go to Madrid," said Billy Leaps.

"Where?"

"Madrid. The Hilton." Billy Leaps hung up.

Cowboy turned to the woman in the bed. She had heard him speak two words: "nothing" and "where."

"I have to go," he said, already rising from the bed.

She'd begged him to stay. She promised her husband's fortune. Her father's too. She'd divorce for Cowboy. Give up the Church and her hope for heaven.

But Cowboy was thinking only of Parkes. So the man had his limits. He hadn't been able to reach Cowboy in Mexico City, though Cowboy had made it as easy as possible.

The woman suddenly lunged out of the bed and grabbed the big automatic out of Cowboy's shoulder holster.

Cowboy thought, *Oh shit it was her . . . she . . .*

But then he realized that she was going to turn it on herself. She wasn't Parkes's agent. She was simply another heartbroken woman. And he hadn't even married her.

He grabbed the gun out of her hand, and held her close while she cried.

The Iberian Airlines jet was speeding across the Atlantic. The stewardesses and the pilots all spoke in Spanish, Cowboy's favorite language—so romantic and soothing. If he worked at it, he could forget he spoke Spanish, and just let the liquid syllables roll over him without imparting their meaning.

But he couldn't do that now. Now while he was in this mood. He willed his body to relax, but it wouldn't. A man who's gone out on point without taking fire takes a long time to come down. It's like cocking a gun and then shelving it for a few months. The tension begins to tear at the mechanism.

Cowboy sat in first class, nearly alone on the overnight flight. He had a stewardess all to himself. She was gorgeous. The black hair was piled high on her head. Her uniform fit so well it looked as if the material had been woven directly on her body. Her smile was dazzling.

She hovered near Cowboy. She took little rests in the seat directly across the aisle from him. She ran her hands over her lap, and then glanced at him. She brushed imaginary lint from her out-jutting breasts. Her fingers lingered there. With the pad of her middle finger she pressed at her nipple through the layers of cloth. She brought his meal, but fumbled with the silverware. The fork dropped down between his legs.

"Excuse me," she said in English, and fished for it.

The back of her hand pressed against his prick. It began instantly to harden. She smiled.

For a while nothing more came of her salacious flirtation. She smiled at him when she took his tray away. A little later she stood beside his seat and reached into the luggage compartment overhead, positioning herself so that her crotch was just at the level of Cowboy's face.

Then, about two hours before their scheduled landing, with the only other occupant of the first-class section asleep, and the curtains drawn that separated them from the tourist class, she once more came to Cowboy's side.

"Señor," she said. Her voice was polite, but her smile was lascivious and unmistakable. She spoke a few sentences in Spanish. Cowboy pretended he didn't understand.

"Sir," she repeated, this time in English, "could you please help me for a moment?"

Cowboy rose from the seat, and carefully adjusted his trousers, as if trying to disguise the hardness there.

The stewardess smiled again. She led him down the aisle to the small, first-class lavatory. She opened the door, and went inside, motioning him to follow. Cowboy grinned expectantly. A Texas grin. He pulled the door closed behind him, and locked it. Still grinning. Already her skirt was up, and her panties were down.

Too fast, sugar.

He let her unzip his pants, move aside his briefs, go for the gold. In the air-conditioned atmosphere of the plane cabin, he was rock-hard and dry. With one hand she pulled him toward her.

"I need you," she whispered, placing his hand down there, pressing his fingers against the wetness. "I need you so bad."

With her other hand, she reached toward her bra. She thought he wouldn't notice.

But he did notice, and he saw the handle of the knife. He measured her response perfectly. Just when she thought she could slice his exposed throat, Cowboy went to work. He stopped the slash of the sharp blade. Then redirected it. Right into her belly.

She drew in her breath sharply. Blood spilled out along the blade of the knife.

Cowboy jerked to one side, to avoid being splashed. They were still very close together in the tiny cubicle. He looked into her eyes, catching her surprised and terrified gaze. The sharp edge of the knife pointed downward. He pushed up on her hand. Unable to resist, the blade slid deeper, up to pierce the heart, tearing the flesh in a harsh line. Touching, extinguishing another life. Another blot on my karma.

Trying his best to stand out of the way of the gushing blood and cursing the ruination of a brand-new pair of pants, Cowboy held her up till he saw that her eyes had glazed over. Then he shoved her down onto the toilet seat and returned to the first-class cabin, leaving an OUT OF ORDER sign prominently on the door.

16

The noise was so familiar that Rosie wondered why he didn't dream about it every night. It was so loud it covered all possibility of speech, and made you think. Or remember. It sent Rosie back, and when he met Harry's eyes and then Applebaum's, he knew they were remembering too. Harry looked even more despondent than usual. He seemed to close his eyes for whole minutes at a time. Rosie looked at him and felt a sympathy. Because Rosie was remembering things too.

This noise—the sound made by a troop-carrying Huey—meant you were going out to the field. Out to try to find the enemy. You hoped you found him fast and you hoped he wasn't waiting patiently just at the place where the helicopter was going to land. Because if he was, he could get you before you had a chance in hell of getting him. Before your feet touched the ground. Rosie had seen it before. Guys put one foot out of the Huey, then froze. Froze because there was a bullet in their brains, and there wasn't anybody home anymore.

Rosie saw the memories in Applebaum's face, too. Asshole though he could be, you had to give the little man credit. He knew they were going into battle. Applebaum understood that. He was cradling that big black M-60, the ammunition belts strapped on his back. He'd used that machine in 'Nam. Applebaum had fired his M-60 maybe more than anyone else in the whole war. He knew every screw of the goddamn weapon. He could change a barrel in his sleep, clear a jam with his teeth if need be. There were times to be grateful you had a lunatic like Applebaum on your side—and that was any time you needed firepower.

Marty held it like it was his lover. It wasn't the first time Rosie had noticed that. Maybe it was his only love. All the talk. All the

110

bragging. Rosie had never seen Marty actually between the sheets with a woman. Everybody had heard the talk beforehand. *I'm gonna get that one.* They had heard the talk afterward. *Best lay a man ever had. Someday I'm gonna go back and find out her name.* Nobody had ever known for sure if the woman even knew Marty existed.

They were swooping downward. Rosie remembered that sensation too. His stomach tightened first, then the rest of his body. His hand automatically charged the rifle, putting a round in the chamber, then went for the trigger.

He hoped to God that their plan worked, because from this point on he was going to be working on pure instinct. The plan was in the back of his mind, and Rosie's legs and hands and eyes and will were going to operate to carry out that plan—but without his ever thinking about it. It was weird. He always wondered, right at this point when he went on automatic pilot, whether this happened to anybody else. But then, when it was all over, he forgot that that's what had occurred, and he never asked.

He looked out the open bay of the helicopter and glanced at the mission hospital below. Strange how different it always looked when you got there. They had been briefed with maps and diagrams. Old aerial photos had been passed around. But it was different now, seeing it below. It was always different. But he still made out the generator station that his group was supposed to take out.

The earth moved up toward them quickly. Then there was sudden contact. They alertly jumped through the door. As planned, Rosie and Applebaum were first. Harry lingered behind. Harry had special work to do.

With gung ho battle cries, Marty and Rosie ran forward a few yards ahead of everyone else. The ground was like soft savanna, dried and crumbling from the drought that had recently infected the area. But even drought-desiccated, it was an oasis in the vast Sahara, with the only known water within a two-hundred-kilometer radius.

The others lagged behind at the choppers, trying to get into their combat order, following their orders to wait for the other helicopters to land.

If I ever saw anybody run ahead like this, Rosie thought, *I'd kill 'em sure. Kill 'em for traitors or fuck-ups*.

But nobody shot them, and Rosie felt contempt for them because of that.

The other Huey began to set down. In the noise and confusion of the landings, no one seemed even to notice the two men who had not followed orders, who had run ahead without waiting for the troops to group. But then Rosie and Applebaum were already out of sight, having dropped to the earth in a small field of sharp, dead grasses. Marty had already set up the M-60 on its bipod.

Rosie gave a nod, and the M-60 sent out the first rounds of its deadly fire. The bullets spat through the air, Marty's sure hand pouring death on the unsuspecting intruders.

The little man's shooting his load, Rosie thought. *Girls, spread your legs*.

The mercs out of the first copter realized they were under fire, but still didn't know from where. The noise of the blades didn't cover the sound of Applebaum's M-60, but it kept the victims from immediately pinpointing the source. So they scattered and fired in all directions.

Rosie would have liked to stay and watch, but he didn't have time. He was moving fast parallel to the line of helicopters, trying to make it look as if he were just ducking for cover. That wasn't hard. Everybody else was.

He aimed the first LAW at the vulnerable belly of the second Huey that had landed. There was a deep shuddering explosion a moment later. That was good, but Rosie didn't have time to judge just how good his handiwork had been. He was setting off the second of the small disposable missiles. And by the time that *boom* began to echo off the first, he was aiming the third.

The plan was very simple. Rosie would take out copters two, three, and four. Applebaum, with the M-60, was to take care of any of the troops who made it out of the copters before Rosie exploded them. Harry, in the first copter, was simply to rope down the pilot—so they'd be able to get out again—and then take up whatever slack Rosie and Marty had left.

Didn't work out quite that way, of course. There were problems. Almost always were.

Amid the smoke and confusion, Rosie could tell that copters

two and three were out. He had to assume that Harry had taken control of number one. That left number four.

And number four was taking off again. The pilot thought he might get away with something. At least the man had sense enough to know the whole operation had been aborted. And he wasn't about to wait for the troops to climb back on. He was going to save his own ass.

Rosie swore as he saw number four rise up off the ground. He fired the last LAW.

Damn! It missed. A few moments later it exploded uselessly a hundred or so yards beyond. Not quite uselessly. It got a man and a woman who were running for cover in that direction. They had become lovers in Parkes's camp. Maybe they had been planning to beg asylum at the convent. Too bad.

No more LAWs. Well, Rosie had trusted his life to his M-16 before. He'd have to do it again. Cowboy had told him to go for the tail rotor. More specifically, to go for where the rotor joined the fuselage. Rosie aimed his rifle and he actually did find a god to pray to as he fired. The noise all around him was deafening. The screams, the gunfire, the helicopter engines and spinning blades. He couldn't know if his aim was good.

Then the helicopter seemed to stall a little. It listed to the left for a few moments. Rosie took his own advice now. He could barely make out the face of the pilot through the glass shield. He aimed for the dark glasses on that shocked white face and pulled the trigger. Got to get that man. That thing makes it back to Major Asshole and it's all over.

The helicopter jumped in midair. What caused that? The pilot? The rotor? Rosie waited. Rosie prayed to that god who had been there just a few seconds ago. Maybe he was hanging around still. The copter lurched hard to the left again and dived fast.

Right toward him.

Rosie ran, jumped, covered his head. All at the same time. That thing had a near full tank of fuel. It was too close. It . . .

BAAAAAMMMMMM!

The hot shards of metal and the gobs of molten glass flew through the air. Something burned Rosie's right forearm. He could even tell its shape as it sank into his flesh—triangular. Something else landed on his right thigh. At first, as it lay on the cloth of his fatigues, it was just warm. But then it got hot all of a sudden. Then it was a branding iron pressed into his flesh. But he couldn't brush it away because he didn't dare take his hands away from his head. There was still more debris in the air. The heavy stuff was falling with potential death all around him. He didn't dare uncover his head. The noise was deafening. He felt the sound of the exploding copter bear down upon him, pressing him into the earth. He felt the hot metal fragments falling onto his body, he even felt the sun high above everything. A blast of unbreathable air, full of flame and burning fuel, roared over his back, and blistered the skin on the backs of his hands, clasped over his head. Rosie smelled his own flesh burning, then he—

Nothing more.

17

Then there was quiet. Suddenly, and unexpectedly, and amazingly, it was quiet. Noise was a memory, and a distant memory at that. The pain was still there, but the heat was different. The heat was all over Rosie now. That was the sun.

He lifted his head. Pain shot through his skull, till it seemed that his head would explode. He dropped his head down again. If they'd take the pain away, he wouldn't mind dying. No headaches in the grave.

"Want me to do something? What do you want me to do, Rosie?"

Get fucked.

Rosie opened his eyes again, slowly this time. He saw the sun. He turned his head. Somebody kicked sand in his face.

"Oh, sorry," said Applebaum.

Fuck Applebaum again. Does he have to kick sand in a dying man's face?

Rosie still couldn't see. He breathed in deeply. Then he realized that was a good sign. No chest wounds. If he didn't have a chest wound, maybe he'd live after all. Despite the headache, Rosie changed his mind. He wanted to wake up tomorrow morning. When he breathed in deep, he smelled death, but it was others' death that stank. Others' deaths, and exploded munitions, and burned fuel. Then something else—something sweet and rare.

Sweet Christ, I'm smelling heaven.

He opened his eyes, and it was a black angel there, a black angel in white robes and a damn peculiar hat.

She said something in a foreign language, and then she ripped open his pants.

Rosie screamed.

Something wet was poured over the wound. It stung. It burned like fire. And then it cooled off. Fast. When Rosie opened his eyes again, he could see.

The woman with the black face was a nun.

From the convent hospital.

Maybe his head and his brain were okay, if he could figure out something like that.

Maybe he wouldn't be a human parsnip, covered with bedsores, stinking of shit, in a bed in a state hospital where they changed the sheets once a month.

Nun had cheekbones, too. Rosie liked cheekbones. Bet she had an ass as high as those cheekbones. Bet under those goddamn robes—

Maybe he was all right down there, too. Sure felt like it.

He heard a ripping sound. He was a medic, and knew the sound. Bandages being stripped.

"No," someone said, and the nurse suddenly disappeared from view.

She protested in the foreign tongue again. French? Must be French. Except it didn't sound like French. What the hell do Belgians speak anyway?

He didn't smell her anymore. He smelled death again. And he smelled someone familiar. Harry. You got to know a man by his sweat. Unique, like fingerprints. You live in a jungle with a man, you can smell him coming. Even though Rosie couldn't see his friend's face, he knew it was Harry kneeling down behind him.

Rosie tried to speak. His mouth wouldn't work right. But Harry knew the question he was going to ask.

"We're all set. Rosie, we got to get back. You get your choice. We can take you with us, or you can stay here at the hospital. Nobody's going to be attacking here for a while. But if we take you back with us, I got to fix you up myself. There's only three of us left, plus the pilot. We can't have you showing up with bandages out of the infirmary here. Like first there was a massacre and then a tea party. We got to do you up with shirts. And we only got a couple of morphine styrettes. Marty shot up the medic."

"Your choice," said Applebaum.

Rosie looked up. On one side of him was Applebaum, grinning for some insane reason, probably because Applebaum grinned at anything. On the other side was the nurse, high cheekbones and all. Goddamn, she even had tits. Concern and sympathy on her face. Whatever that language was, he liked the sound of it in her mouth. Either Applebaum or else the white robes, a clean bed, a hovering nurse—what a choice.

No choice. He thought of Beeker. And Parkes.

"Let's go," he murmured.

"What?" said Applebaum.

But Harry had heard, and a moment later Rosie felt himself lifted up and carried off. His head tilted one way and then another, but on every side he saw smoking carnage, bloodied bodies, scorched grass, everything illuminated by a pitiless noontime desert sun.

The nurse ran alongside, still protesting in that sweet, sweet language.

He felt pain in a dozen places. He even tried counting his words, but as soon as he got up to five, number one or number two would reassert itself like a stiletto stab, and he'd have to start counting again with that one because it hurt most.

Harry held him in his arms for a moment, while Applebaum climbed into the only remaining copter. Rosie looked at the nurse, and engineered a smile.

"Sorry about the mess," he mumbled, and reached out to touch her. But he missed, then Harry hit him with a styrette and it was very quiet again.

The Greek listened to Applebaum, but his worried eyes were on the wounded, unconscious black man. Marty was going a mile a minute. Harry was tightening Rosie's makeshift bandages.

"Man, we sure as hell did it, didn't we, Harry? Huh? Man, that M-60 just sang for me. Bop-bop-bop-bop-bop-bop. They dropped like flies. Man, we got 'em good. That was some hot shit we pulled. Out there, forty-six of 'em, right, did you count? Forty-six. Shooting away with no cover. Almost no cover. Hot shit. Hey, when Rosie went down and you kicked in—that was great."

Harry didn't talk about the part he had played. Or remind Marty that the blond man would have been dead if Ascham's troops hadn't been caught in the cross fire that included Harry's own machine gun.

But Applebaum was right about one thing. It was total success. He and Marty had been the only ones to know what the series of loud explosions was. The ones that ripped through the fuel tanks of the helicopters and created instant ovens for those few members of the squads who had been dumb enough to seek cover in or under the choppers.

All Major Ascham's crack troops had died, most of them in ignorance of what was happening. It was the only death that Harry really feared—to die in confusion, not knowing the manner or the reason for your death. Just as the troops had been told to do, they had lined up a few thousand yards from the targeted hospital. They had stood there, perfect targets from front and back, a series of bowling pins waiting for the ball to roll them over. And he and Marty had had enough 7.62-mm little black balls for all the standing pins.

Then the explosions as Rosie had gone down the line firing the LAWs. He was a good man, had to admit that. Carried those heavy disposable LAWs like they were pick-up sticks. Took out the second and third copters right off, and brought down the fourth with his rifle.

It wasn't pleasant, what that place looked like when Harry and Marty and Rosie got through with it. Not pleasant up close, and not pleasant from up above, when Harry looked down. Black smoke, blood in the dry yellow grass, the only living things there the half dozen nuns in white, with wide wimples, staring up into the sky at the retreating helicopter.

They hadn't understood what had happened, of course. And nobody had tried to explain it to them. But those Ursulines had gone through nearly a century and a half of border conflicts. That fifty more dead had been deposited on their doorstep probably wouldn't even cause them to reschedule their daily prayers.

Marty kept on going, no stopping him, never was a way to keep him quiet. Death did to Marty what coke used to do for Cowboy—made him jovial, made him talkative, made him the buddy of anybody who had managed to survive. Marty was just another burden for Harry. Like the burden of hoping that those wounds that made Rosie bleed so bad were just superficial. Like making sure that the pilot—the only man to survive the massacre—kept on course, and didn't try any funny business with the radio.

"Man, I feel great. Just great! We really pulled it off. We really took them. Assholes never even thought there'd be somebody in their own ranks that'd take 'em out. They were expecting nuns with slingshots, I bet. Fucking nuns with baseball bats and razor blades."

All the time Marty was talking, his M-60, his gargantuan machine gun, was pointed at the head of the surviving pilot. That had been Harry's first assignment. Get to the pilot of the number one copter and secure him. Knock him out, tie him up, make sure he lived. They had to have a way back to the camp. Then Harry did the next thing on his list. He had taken his M-60 to the open bay of the helicopter and, as soon as he heard the first shot of Marty's weapon, he had joined in the attack.

They had killed forty-six men. Marty was right about the number. Only had one more to go.

It pained Harry to prepare for this next death. So many things pained Harry. But especially after seeing the nuns . . .

The look of horror on their faces when they had run up from the portals of the convent, to see the strewn, bleeding meat that was forty-six human beings who had all been alive five minutes before. And the look on their faces when they had seen Harry and Applebaum rise up. They didn't understand what had happened, but they knew who had done the killing. They looked away from Harry and Marty. They went systematically among the dead, looking for any sign of life. That one, the one who found Rosie, she was a real spiritual person, you could tell from the concern in her face. She had known Harry had caused all those deaths. She probably thought he was planning to finish off Rosie too. He wished he had had time to stop and explain.

There never was time.

Civilians never understood, anyway. Even if you did stop and explain.

And now, without even being able to try to give that explanation—to say to that nice black nun in the starched white robes, *We did it to save you and the others, to protect the hospital, to stop a very evil man from doing even worse*—Harry was already having to plan the death of another man.

"Bop-bop-bop-bop-bop-bop . . . Your machine and my machine, they were right in rhythm. Didn't you hear it, Harry? Didn't you just love it? Talk about music! Talk about a quarter in the jukebox! And man, didn't that music play!"

"Yeah, Marty. Real music." They had been flying three quarters of an hour. The pilot was drenched in sweat. He couldn't have talked into the radio even if Applebaum had thrown the M-60 out the open bay. Major Ascham's camp came into view below.

"Now, asshole." Marty lifted the nozzle of the M-60. "You do it just like we said and it'll be okay. We let you live. Like we said, we were ambushed by Bashi soldiers. They were waiting. Somebody must have tipped 'em off. Security leak somewhere. Somebody squealed. We're the lucky ones that got away. You *comprende*?"

The terrified pilot nodded. If he had wanted to be a hero, Harry thought, he could have downed the chopper back in the desert, hoped maybe he lived and we didn't. But he decided to string out his hope, and carry us all the way back to camp. Hope was a funny thing, Harry had decided long ago. Sometimes it was the enemy.

The pilot brought the helicopter into the space directly over the landing area. Little men—they looked little from this height—ran like stick figures toward the strip, probably wondering why there was only one returning alone.

Harry felt the earth come closer. He sensed the jerk of the landing. The pilot was automatically reaching for the switch that would disengage the motor. That was when Harry reached around and fired two shots from a silenced 9-mm right through the pilot's chest.

Marty calmly reached forward and pressed the switch himself. The blades slowed. The noise dropped. Maybe the silencer wouldn't have been necessary while the blades were still going. Maybe. But no chances.

Harry quickly removed the silencer and shoved it in his pants. Stuffing the pistol back into his pack, he moved to the open door and shouted, "Wounded! We got wounded!"

18

Beeker had been living the days of the past week in a burning passion. It was as though he were back in 'Nam. As though the battle for Khe Sahn were going to take place tomorrow—only this time he knew about it. He was at peak and he maintained it day after day, till it felt that the peak itself was like a mountain of glass, threatening to shiver itself into a million fragments of uselessness at any moment.

He patrolled the farm with all the trained stealth of a Marine and with all the inherited instinct of a Cherokee. He went over every inch of the place every day, looking for signs of intrusion that the electronic surveillance system hadn't picked up. He found only Cowboy's own equipment, but he remained always alert for anything else. Anything out of place. Parkes might come after the boy again.

He had sent Cowboy to Madrid, getting him nearer Libya by degrees. He'd join Cowboy in Spain.

Cowboy had been tailed. A stewardess on the plane. Parkes's net was wide. Would it be thrown over the farm and Tsali again, though? And if so, when?

Parkes had burned Beeker's home, tried to kill him and the others—but worst of all, he had threatened Beeker's son.

That was why Beeker was at peak. Because of Tsali.

He saw the concern on Tsali's face. He had to ignore it. Everything had to be done right, and Beeker found himself yelling at the kid. He drove the boy, all the time, making him spend double hours on the shooting range, getting angry if Tsali's aim was less than marksman perfect. Beeker ran him all over the farm, ambushing him when he could, forcing the kid to set up ambushes that Beeker always spotted and tore up. He made the kid figure a hundred ways to the bunker—plans for an attack by three, five, thirty men. He tried to pour a war's worth of experience into the kid's head and knew it could never stick.

His life depends on it.

They ate in silence, quick tasteless meals. They searched the farm again and again, ran more each day, spent longer hours on the range with the M-16.

"I know it's hard," Billy Leaps finally said, one night late, when he too was exhausted.

It's the way a warrior must be, Tsali signed.

Tsali went on every patrol. He ran as far and as fast as Beeker. The firing of the M-16, the constant vigilance—it was the daily routine. A routine with only a single moment of relief.

That was at night, after their dinner, after Tsali had checked the functioning of the computers, after the two men had cleaned and reloaded their rifles to be placed on the floor beside their cots, ready to be taken up in an instant—that was when Tsali signed "Good night" to Billy Leaps at the door of his room. For a single moment, in Tsali's eyes, Beeker would see a weary, too-young, frightened boy. A single moment of vulnerability that Tsali reserved for his father and admitted only to him.

Good night.

Then the phone finally rang.

It was only then that Billy Leaps realized that he had been waiting for it.

He sat bolt upright in the bed. Five A.M.

"I'm not used to claling men at five A.M.," she said. He could see her smile. "But I think it must be the only time you're in the house."

At peak Beeker couldn't let that twinge have its effect on his body. Not even the rounded syllables of Delilah's voice could bring him back.

"What's going on?" he asked in a voice that stated clearly that he had no interest in the amenities.

She didn't protest. She was a professional too. "Parkes is moving into Bashi. It seems obvious now, I don't know why our people didn't figure it out before. His camp is only a few

122

hundred kilometers away from the disputed border. We have information that he's already planning a major raid on one of the border encampments—a mission hospital, as a matter of fact.''

"Bashi hasn't got shit," said Beeker. "What's he want with a country like that? No oil, no copper, no—"

Delilah interrupted him. "All the better for him in that case. Nobody will care when he takes it over, because nobody wants the damn place. All Parkes is after is the country itself—its sovereign status. Its seat in the United Nations. Its power to borrow money from Western banks. He'd be able to auction off rights to an air base, to us, or to the Russians, for instance—or to anybody'd who'll pay more. Owning your own country has practically endless possibilities for a greedy, unscrupulous man.''

"It's black, though," said Beeker. "Are they gonna let a white man in at the top? Don't they have a king or something?"

"Yes," replied Delilah. "The third son of a tribal chief, who was appointed to the monarchy when Belgium gave the country its independence. Not much of a lineage there. This third son—Om-batu—spent ten days at a hotel in Oxford so he now considers himself the country's most educated man. And may well be. Bashi has a lot of problems. But a year ago Om-batu's father died. And instead of turning over the succession to the eldest son, they put in a moderate military man. Sons revolted, and the two eldest died. Om-batu fled the country, and Parkes got hold of him. That moderate military man, to everybody's surprise, is doing all right. He's already started to put in reforms, and he'll put in more, if the Western banks will lend him a little money. And so on, and so on," Delilah concluded hastily. "I don't want to go into all this now. The details are written out, and they've been delivered to Mr. Hatcher in Madrid." Beeker was surprised for a moment—how had she known where Cowboy was? "What I have to say to you is, Parkes has got to be stopped from taking over Bashi by reinstating the king."

"Parkes will never get to Bashi," Beeker vowed.

"He's there now," said Delilah.

Beeker was ready to go in half an hour.

He stood by the pickup truck and hesitated. He was trying to find the words he should speak to Tsali.

The boy was standing close by, himself trapped because he wanted to do *something*. He felt foolish. He didn't know how to stand at attention and salute the way a Marine would. He didn't know the old ways, the manner in which a warrior would say farewell and godspeed to another warrior. He didn't know . . . and he broke. All the emotions he was trying to shape into a ritual good-bye spilled open inside him. He lurched forward and wrapped his arms around Beeker's waist. Tsali squeezed as hard as he could. He squeezed, then stepped back, instantly embarrassed and ashamed by his show of affection. This wasn't how two men . . .

But Beeker's arms came around Tsali's shoulders and gently held him for a moment. Tsali stood back, head high, proud of the man who cared enough to keep him—proud of the man Beeker wanted him to be.

Beeker's right hand rested on Tsali's shoulder. "I'll be back."

Then the Black Beret leader got into the pickup truck and drove off down the long driveway.

Tsali waited until all sight and sound of the vehicle had disappeared. Then he went back into the house and retrieved his M-16. It was time to patrol the perimeter again.

19

Rosie was sitting in a bed in the temporary field hospital. Strange to think in terms of mercenary doctors and nurses, but here they were. An Italian team, though Rosie never did figure out how they got involved, but Parkes knew the troops would never fight without some hope of surviving the inevitable wounds. So, somehow, there were doctors.

The white bandages wrapped around Rosie in so many places were in startling contrast to the blackness of his skin. The wounds had been superficial. Lots of bleeding, not much else. There'd be scars of course. To go with the ones he already had from 'Nam. Scars show up differently on a black man, a not very pretty pink against the rich chocolate flesh. The scars didn't bother Rosie. They told him where he'd been. And he remembered being surprised that the scars didn't bother most women either. Some of them really liked them.

"This is our hero!" Major Asshole's voice interrupted Rosie's dreams. The idiot had bought their story. How they had been ambushed themselves, betrayed by someone in the camp. How it was a miracle that the three of them had gotten out alive. How the suffering pilot had heroically flown them to safety and then died of the two bullets he had received in the battle. And nobody ever figured out that that poor guy hadn't been shot till that copter set down on the landing strip. If Ascham was good at anything it was seeing what he wanted to see, and not seeing anything else at all.

Next to Ascham stood a big, fat black man.

What a gut on that one, Rosie thought. How many people went hungry to produce that basketball of extra flesh? In sub-Saharan Africa you showed a fat gut the way you show a stuffed wallet in

Vegas. The man was wearing some kind of tribal robes. Years before, Rosie might have been impressed by that shit. Before he discovered you could buy that kind of fabric in J.C. Penney's. Before he did a little history reading.

A while back—about the time the Revolution was spreading through Newark, and Newark was burning down—Rosie had bought the line that blacks had been torn from idyllic Africa by ravenous white slavers. That the blacks of America had been ripped from their proud and noble homes by those evil white ghosts. But then Rosie got to reading and began to understand how many of the blacks had been captured and sold to the slavers by other blacks, often their own tribesmen. Rosie never looked at a native African the same way again. They weren't his brothers. They were the ones who had sold Rosie's ancestors into slavery. He never let the superficiality of a shared race and skin interfere with the contempt he felt for that ancient betrayal.

"This is the prince," Ascham said officiously. "Prince Om-batu."

"Prince?"

"The heir presumptive to the throne of Bashi."

The fat black man stood momentarily prouder, but the weight of his belly was too much for him to keep propped up. He let his waist sag back down to the low orb that gravity defined. "We are proud of the ferocity of our troops in attacking the mission hospital."

"The principal training ground and ammunition depot of the antiroyalist forces," Ascham gently corrected.

"Yes," agreed the black man readily. "I am commissioning a medal to be made up for the three survivors. I am designing it myself. I will pin it on myself. I will make you my field marshal."

"Field marshal of what?" Rosie demanded.

"My armies."

"These jokers?" With a contemptuous wave of his bandaged hand Rosie indicated a knot of the mercenaries just then passing outside the tent.

"No, no, certainly not," said the Prince, exchanging a slightly uneasy glance with Ascham. "These valiant warriors are our

126

allies." The distinction seemed important, at least in the fuddled mind of Om-batu. "Right now, my armies are under false leadership, treacherous leadership. By a lieutenant of my father's former honor guards. But when the land of my father, and my father's people, is once again under my imperial rule, you will be field marshal. With many medals."

Something had become clear to Rosie. The attack on the hospital had not simply been a favor done by Parkes for Colonel Qadhafi. It was Parkes's own target as well. Maybe Qadhafi had better things to think about than a bunch of Ursuline nuns in the desert—though Qadhafi, always on the lookout for somebody innocent to kill, couldn't have found a greater concentration of innocence than down there in that desert-bleached hospital and convent. It was apparent, at any rate, that Parkes's goal was to reestablish the monarchy in Bashi. And Rosie even had a pretty good guess why Parkes would take the trouble to interfere in the internal squabbles of such a nothing piece of real estate as Bashi. Bashi to the south was all impenetrable rain forest; to the north it was the driest desert in Africa. In the middle was a narrow strip of parched savanna and pestilential swampland where twenty or thirty million undernourished blacks lived out their miserable existences. With Om-batu as their titular, exiled king, and a lieutenant in the honor guards—about the level of a weaponless security officer back home, Rosie guessed—actually running the government, Rosie knew why Parkes was interested in a place like that. It would be pretty easy to be the power behind any throne that Prince Om-batu was seated on.

Play along, Rosie thought to himself. *Maybe you can get close enough to that throne to reach behind it and drag Parkes out by the throat.*

"I'm told you will fully recover," said Om-batu.

"He suffered severely on your behalf, Prince, but luckily all his wounds were superficial."

"About six pints of blood, about fifty stitches, nearly lost my left eye—but nothing for you to worry about." Then at the end he added, without a trace of the contempt he felt, "Sire."

The Prince smiled a brilliant smile of condescension on Rosie.

"Prince," said Rosie, "I sure would like the opportunity to take

127

part in this. I sure would like to go. I sure would like to fight at your side. Am I gonna have time to recover from my wounds before you go in? That's all I wanna know."

I'd make a pretty good house boy, Rosie thought, inwardly convulsed with laughter. *Bowing and scraping to master. Waiting on table, and licking up crumbs off the floor.*

"The details of the invasion are not yet set," said Om-batu, waving away the objection that Ascham was making.

Good, thought Rosie. *I'm learning something, 'cause Major Asshole wants him to shut up.*

"Well, I sure would like to go along. I sure would be happy if I could help you to restore the throne of my ancestors."

"Were your people from Bashi?" asked the Prince, in pleased astonishment.

"Near as I can tell," said Rosie. And it might be true, after all.

"Well then," said the Prince, "I think it is very important that you come along to assist. You will go with me, Abdul Muhamed. I will ask Prime Minister Parkes if he will not postpone the invasion until—"

Ascham laid his commoner's hand sharply on the Prince's arm. "Prince, please . . ."

Prime Minister Parkes. Hot damn. I was right. Prime Minister Woodrow Wilson Parkes. Rosie grinned at the Prince. *Man, I knew you was a fool. But there's one man in the whole wide world ain't never gonna be Prime Minister of Shit when I'm done, and that man is Woodrow Wilson Parkes.*

Within two days, against the advice of the Italian doctor, Rosie was up and about. He picked at the stitches, and the scars were still an angry red, but he wasn't going to chance missing out on Parkes because of a little unhealed flesh.

He wandered slowly around the camp, as if getting his legs again, but in reality to see what had happened since he was out of commission. One thing impressed him—there were already replacements for the fifty who had died at the Ursuline mission. The quality wasn't as high, of course, but the bodies were there. He was also on the lookout for other spies, such as himself, such as Luc St. Jean. He'd like to warn them away, if he could. But he didn't see any likely subjects. Either the plants weren't there, or they were so well-disguised as mindless idiots that Rosie couldn't detect them.

It wasn't so hard to find time to talk to Harry. It was to be expected that the three lone survivors of the border raid would have become comrades after their experience. Still, Rosie didn't like to push it. He talked to Harry as they stood beneath adjoining showers. The noise of the falling tepid water covered what they said.

"They got Fokkers," said Harry without preamble, turning beneath the water, and not even looking at Rosie. "You know those Dutch planes? NATO uses 'em for paratroopers."

Rosie whistled, but low and soft. "Going first-class this time."

"So they got 'em all up in the sky, practicing. Everybody's got to jump. They're all eating it up—least the ones who don't shit in their pants are—making believe they're storm troopers. Ascham wants to go in low and fast. If we don't kill 'em, the jump probably will."

"Marty?"

"Head instructor," sighed Harry. "Gets to jump five, six times a day. Screams at 'em if they don't yell '*Geronimo*' when they bail out. Pig heaven for Marty."

"They're gonna take over Bashi," said Rosie. "Parkes is already Prime Minister. The fat nigger you see walking around in orange and yellow all the time, that's the Crown Prince. We're all gonna drop in and liberate Bashi. And put that joker on the top of the heap."

Harry thought about this for a bit. "Think we ought to try to get word to Billy Leaps? What do we do if we don't hear from him? Or Cowboy. I look every day, I ain't seen Cowboy. And I've been sort of expecting him. He could have fun with a Fokker. Said he liked 'em one time."

Others were waiting in line for the shower. Harry turned off the water and grabbed the sheet he had taken off his cot. That's all there was for towels. Didn't matter though. Sheets dried pretty fast in this climate. Rosie remained beneath the falling tepid water. "We can't take a chance on getting information

129

out. We got to do what looks best to us. That's all. That's what Beeker'd expect. Right?"

Harry just nodded, and walked off.

"And take on the whole goddamn Bashi Imperial Army and marching drum corps," said Rosie under his breath.

20

Cowboy answered the knock on the hotel door. It was Beeker.

"Anybody contact you yet?" the Black Beret leader demanded.

"Hello to you too. Yes, the past few days here have been real nice. No, nobody's tried to kill me yet this morning."

"Shut up, Cowboy! Has anybody contacted you yet?" Beeker threw the single bag he carried onto the bed. "They should have."

"Yeah," said Cowboy, giving up. "Got a call. Not for me. For you. Somebody's expecting you. Come on, Beeker, you're my pal, you're my old buddy. Don't you want to hear—"

"Tsali gave me the message you sent. Stewardess tried to off you. You offed her. You're pissed off that a new pair of pants got a little bloodstain around the cuffs. More— knowing you—you're pissed off you didn't get into her pants first."

"You're a hard man, Billy Leaps Beeker. You're a man who's got granite for a heart, when it comes to his old friends."

But the comment at least got the smile onto the leader's face. "Okay, Cowboy, I'm sorry. Transatlantic flight. And I'm beginning to smell Parkes. That's—"

"I know, Beeker, I know. Kid okay?"

"Fine."

"Thanks for the amenities. Yes, there's a message. All CIA secret type. Some unnamed dude wants a rendezvous with you. Code words and dark alleys."

"How'm I supposed to meet him?"

"He's calling back. He'll set it up."

They relaxed as well as they could, Beeker sprawled out on the bed, trying to get his muscles in tune with European time. There was a great deal the two men could have said to one another, but they were silent. This may have been a hotel room in the Hilton, and when they looked out of the window what they saw was the towers of the city's cathedral, but Billy Leaps and Cowboy both knew that the place might be dangerous.

At last Beeker spoke. "Goddamn everybody knows we're here. Delilah's people. The CIA. Parkes too, I suppose. Did you get that stuff about Bashi?"

"Know more than I want to know about that damn place," said Cowboy. "Stuff's over there. Later, I'll show you what's important."

"Everything's important," said Billy Leaps. "You never know what's going to be useful. So you learn everything."

"Right," said Cowboy, then they lapsed into silence again.

The phone rang about an hour after that. Beeker answered. Some voice—obviously, and Beeker thought ridiculously, attempting to disguise itself—tried to set up a clandestine meeting in some remote suburb of Madrid. It would necessitate Beeker renting a car, getting a map from a certain gas-station attendant, driving by a particular route, giving a code word to "Manuel" at a junkyard—and so on forever.

"Listen," said Beeker, interrupting, "you want to meet me? Cowboy and I'll be in the lobby bar at the Hilton in an hour."

They knew him at once. That idiotic uniform CIA types wore like a badge. He stood in the doorway to the empty hotel bar and looked around. Beeker and Cowboy were sipping mineral water—at Beeker's insistence. Cowboy was surprised he spotted them so quickly. Just 'cause they were the only Americans in the place, just 'cause Beeker had his torn ear turned toward the man and looked just like what he was—a battle-scarred Marine, and just 'cause Cowboy wore a pair of aviator sunglasses and a hat that read GO TEXAS AGGIES didn't mean that the CIA would have enough evidence to proceed on. Usually you had to wear a sign across your chest, maybe one that glowed or flashed, to get the message across. But the guy made his way across the room and took a seat without asking. Maybe this one's IQ was higher than a squashed possum's—but Cowboy still had his doubts. CIA was CIA.

"It's not the best idea to meet this way."

"I'm Beeker. This is Cowboy. This is a fine place to meet. Comfortable. They speak the language here. And we're leaving as soon as we've finished with you." He pointed to the two packed bags sitting alongside the table. "What you got for us?"

The man grimaced at the quick, bald beginning. "I'm Sam Jacobson. I wish they'd set up some code word, something that—"

Beeker waved away the man's discomfort. "They didn't. Come off it. We know who you are. You know us. What you got to show?"

Jacobson actually wasn't as bad a looking guy as most CIA operatives. He had a little character to his face, a few lines, a couple of gestures that indicated he might know how to use his fist for something other than signing travel expense forms. Cowboy found his usual disdain for the CIA easing a little bit. But not much. After all, this was just one guy.

Jacobson put his briefcase on the small cocktail table. He looked around to see if they were observed. Not unless the fourteen-year-old boy with a broom in the distant corner had trained a listening device on them. It was half-past ten in the morning, and nobody was drinking yet. They were all still having breakfast on the other side of the lobby. Jacobson at last opened the case and withdrew a large manila envelope. He handed it to Beeker then replaced his case on the floor beside him.

The waitress came over, and Jacobson very uncomfortably ordered a glass of orange juice.

Beeker undid the wire clasp and pulled out the contents. A set of aerial photographs. "Parkes's base?" Beeker asked.

Jacobson nodded his head, yes.

Beeker put the prints on the table between himself and Cowboy so they could both study them. They sifted through the glossy sheets of paper. Jacobson got up and went to the bar for the orange juice he ordered. He didn't want the waitress to see the photographs. When he returned, the photographs were already back in their envelope. "Nothing for us," said Cowboy. Beeker nodded to agree.

"Anything else?" the leader asked.

Jacobson was distressed. "What do you mean—nothing for

you? That's Parkes's base of operations right there. That's where you start.''

''Is Parkes there?'' Beeker demanded. He knew where Parkes was. Delilah had told him. He was already in Bashi.

''No. He's already in Bashi-Bruges. That's the capital city. But he has only a very small force with him. Evidently they're going to drop right on top of the army barracks there and spread out from there to secure some other positions. The radio station, we imagine—there's only one. But this camp is his main base of operations.''

''No it ain't,'' Cowboy said slowly. He took a sip of mineral water, and for the hundredth time cursed Billy Leaps for not letting a man have a decent glass of scotch. ''We got some people there. Consider that base of operations null and void.''

''You have a force there already?'' Jacobson was incredulous. Beeker's assent was silent.

''How large? We've got that camp pegged for at least three hundred, including support people. They have planes, some light artillery. You couldn't possibly—''

''We've got enough men there to take 'em out,'' said Beeker, then seemed to dismiss that whole issue. ''Now, Mr. Hatcher here and I are going to Bashi-Bruges. To take care of Parkes. Personally. So what can you tell us about the situation there?''

Jacobson took a deep breath. ''It's not that we love the regime there now. Hardly. A leftist regime that's got enough guts and gumption to keep out the Cubans—but that's about it. They're certainly not friendly to us.''

''Us?'' echoed Cowboy, with a grin.

Jacobson cleared his throat. ''The country's headed by a man named Jamad. Mother black, father Arab. Right now, there's no terror—that we know of. No great atrocities. At any rate it's not what it was like under the previous ruler—the Emperor. Jamad is the visionary type. Speeches and piety. Refuses to take sides between us and the Russians. All for land reform, reforestation, that sort of thing. Doesn't want a whole lot of American dollars invested because he fears influence. Worried about—''

''Worried about his people,'' Cowboy said, quickly downing his mineral water. His opinion of the CIA had just dipped again. Sam Jacobson was mouthing the sentiments of Thomas Jefferson as if they were left-wing sedition.

The agent understood he'd been shut off. He changed subjects. "In any event, Jamad hasn't invested anything in the army. Sent all the soldiers south and north of the capital to work on land development."

"Beat their swords into plowshares, huh?" Cowboy grinned.

"Something like that," Jacobson agreed reluctantly. "But it cannot be considered a wise move. Because now the country's military is pitifully underarmed and undermanned. That's the real problem. Just Parkes's two hundred fifty, three hundred, well-armed troops could take over. Take the capital and you've got the country. He'd have the place for his own. And *nobody* wants that."

"He's there now? For certain?" Beeker's eyes were burning bright now. Jacobson winced at their unnatural light.

"We're still putting the pieces together," said Jacobson. "But Parkes is definitely in Bashi-Bruges. In league with General Da-goman, who is the head of the Bashi Army. We don't think that this Da-goman has ever bought Jamad's reformist line. It isn't in his blood to do that. He'd like to see the royal line back on the throne. We suspect he's the local key to Parkes's plan. And that's all we know right now. During the reign of the Emperor we had someone there, actually in the army, but he died. We're not even sure how. Now we have to depend on the radio broadcasts, newspaper reports, interviews with people who have visited there—it takes time to train someone and get them in place. We have to—"

"Right," said Beeker, cutting off Jacobson's complaint. All CIA men eventually got around to the bellyache. It's probably what they did best. At any rate they did a lot of it. Billy Leaps threw some Spanish bills on the table and led Cowboy out. They had a plane to catch.

Jacobson sat at the table with the photographs that these men hadn't even bothered to take with them. As he sipped his orange juice he wondered how these very strange men from the States had ever managed to infiltrate Parkes's camp. He wondered how many of Parkes's three hundred men they had on their side, to be so confident of victory. Forty, fifty, at least. At the very least.

Jacobson had obviously never met Applebaum.

135

21

Prince Om-batu had the biggest structure in the compound handed over to him. It was only a prefabricated plywood building, but it had real doors and windows. It kept out the sun during the day and the dust-laden wind at night. There was even an airconditioner. The Prince never turned it off. Om-batu and his few retainers lived in an opulence that contrasted starkly with the spartan existence of the mercenaries. It seemed only appropriate to the Prince that there be an honor guard, a small select force to protect his royal person.

And who better than the three survivors of the border raid, the three men who had proved themselves the first heroes in the Prince's cause? Abdul Muhamed and his two friends.

Ascham should have fought the idea of having Rosie, Applebaum, and the Greek as the Prince's honor guard. He shouldn't have been willing to give up three genuine fighting men in this large untested force—especially since the only ones with guts enough to volunteer for action had been slaughtered back at the mission hospital. That's why Rosie decided that Ascham wanted to have the Prince watched very carefully. He wanted to know just what the Prince was going to do, who he was going to see, and when.

Harry pointed out something else to Rosie—that there was a large safe hidden beneath a mass of material and boxes at the back of the Prince's quarters. There was no need to have a safe, and to hide it, if there was nothing of value inside. Harry and Rosie both suspected that within that safe was the money—probably stolen from the people of Bashi—that was financing this operation. Which meant not only was Parkes planning to get his own country, he was engineering that usurpation with somebody else's cash.

The Prince had wanted new uniforms for his three bodyguards, and had even drawn sketches of them. He showed them proudly.

They were to wear yellow turbans, open khaki shirts with a tiger-pattern scarf at the neck, broad leather belts across their chests, and—

"A skirt!" screamed Applebaum. "A fucking skirt!"

The Prince drew back, offended.

"It ain't a skirt," said Harry quickly. "It's—I don't know what you call it—but it's what the warriors in this part of the world have always worn, it's—"

"I ain't wearing a fucking skirt for the King of Siam!" Marty was jumping up and down on the oriental carpet before the wide-bottomed chair that served the Prince in Exile as throne.

Rosie took a deep breath.

"What he means, Your Highness, is that he feels we would be a more effective force for Your Majesty if we remained in our uniforms, as we are now—"

The Prince began to protest, but Rosie didn't let him speak. He went on hastily, using his deferential retainer voice, "We are used to these uniforms, Sire, and because we are used to them, we'll be more effective in them. We've killed many men wearing these clothes, your highness. That should count for something. Yassir Arafat—you know him, of course—"

The Prince nodded eagerly. He had seen Arafat on television many times, but he didn't tell Rosie that was the extent of his acquaintance with the head of the Palestinian Liberation Organization.

"—Yassir Arafat has a bodyguard composed of seven or eight large men—blond, Scandinavian, Aryan types. They don't wear uniforms that suggest the PLO, they wear uniforms that remind people of their origins, in Prussia and northern Germany. They are more effective that way. Yassir Arafat's bodyguards are not Palestinian, they don't try to look Palestinian. That's what our friend here was saying, wasn't it?"

"Sure," said Marty, who was still rising up and down on his toes in distress. Harry had had to take the drawing away to keep Marty from ripping it up.

"Yes," said the Prince, "you will keep your uniforms. On one condition."

"No condi—" sputtered Marty.

"What condition, Your Highness?" said the Greek, pushing Marty away with a light backhand.

"That you kill many many more men in my name, and for my honor."

Rosie, Harry, and Marty exchanged quick glances. Then all three smiled.

"Yes, Your Highness," said Rosie politely.

Even if they hadn't been assigned to the Prince's tent, the Black Berets would have figured out what was going on. It was obvious that the operation against Bashi demanded a minimal level of troops. They were still waiting to bring that number up, at least to replace the number lost at the border hospital, and very probably to go higher.

Ascham wasn't making any secret about waiting for his three hundred "usables" to be ready. Rosie and Harry heard the news every afternoon when he came to share whiskey-laced tea with the Prince. More whiskey than tea. The news was censored, of course, but with what Major Asshole said, what they themselves had seen, what Applebaum had heard from the other troops—he was still conducting paratroop lessons—they had a pretty good idea of what the real story was.

The Black Berets were only waiting. Alertly, but without nervousness. They had been through too much, separately and together, and what all that had taught them was to trust their instincts. Their instincts would tell them when the time was right. Up until then, they just had to be careful. You had to be on the lookout for the unexpected, for the thing that could wreck your carefully laid plans. There was always something.

This time, Applebaum brought news of it. The thing that could screw them up. One afternoon, when the time for action seemed like it might come very quickly now, he ran up to Rosie, all out of breath.

"Slow down," said Rosie in a low voice, afraid that Applebaum's excitement might alarm the Prince inside. "Slow down, Asshole. Can't be that important."

138

"Is though. Two of the replacements. I know 'em. They know me."

"Where from?" said Harry, standing on the other side of the narrow door that was the entrance to the Prince's quarters.

" 'Nam."

"Americans?" asked Rosie.

"SEALs."

"Shit," Harry whispered.

"You know 'em too," said Applebaum to his friend. "Mason and Dozier. Those red-necks from Florida."

"Them! They still together?"

"Never could pry 'em apart," said Marty. "Something weird about that, if you ask me."

"Nobody asked you," said Rosie, who had been thinking. "Listen, you guys, we're not exactly inconspicuous here. If those two guys know you, then they're gonna meet up with you. And they don't know we're under assumed names. So all that adds up to—we got to get to them first. Harry, you go. Marty, you take over."

Marty and Harry obeyed like Rosie was speaking with Billy Leaps Beeker's voice. Marty gave directions to the tent where Mason and Dozier were billeted, and then took up the Greek's station on the other side of the door.

"What do I say?" Harry asked.

"Play it," said Rosie. "That's all. You'll figure out what has to be done."

Harry was off. Rosie turned to Marty to say, "All right. What's the story on these guys?"

"Absolute assholes," said Marty. But he began every description that way. It didn't mean much. "Think they're God's gift to Women, War, and America. Harry and I went through SEALs training with them at Great Lakes. Major assholes. Gave Harry a real hard time."

Marty's eyes shifted away.

Gave you a pretty hard time, too, I bet, thought Rosie.

"And you're sure they'll know Harry when he goes up to 'em? You sure they'd remember you?"

"They'll remember. They got reason to remember. Harry and me one time . . . They said something, and we . . ."

"Got the picture," said Rosie.

Harry walked right up to their tent and squatted down on his haunches. Two men peered out suspiciously.

Harry remembered them, just like Marty had. Two guys, never apart. One with red hair and freckles. The other a dirty blond, always sunburned. One of 'em was Mason, the other Dozier, but since they were always together nobody had ever bothered to figure out which was which. They were just a team, that's all. Mason & Dozier.

Then they recognized Harry too. Their suspicion changed to something else. Hate. Never forgot a face they didn't like.

"Fuck off, Greek," said one of them. The red-haired one. Nice greeting after ten years.

"The hairy Greek," sneered the other. "You still braid the hair on your balls?"

"What are you guys doing out here?" Harry asked.

"Got us a contract. Cash up front and the payment's in gold. We like that. Paying in fucking gold," said the blond one. Mason or Dozier. Who the hell knew which one? "What are you doing here?"

Harry didn't answer.

"You still got that Jew hanging on your belt? What was that little fucker's name? Applebutt? Assholebaum? Some fucking Jew name . . ."

"Marty's here," said Harry. "But he's under another name. So am I. So when you see us, don't use the old names. Got it?"

Mason and Dozier grinned and laughed. All Harry could see of them was two faces peering out of the open tent flap. They had lost some more teeth.

"We got it," they snickered.

"But don't blame us if we forget," sneered the blond one. "Don't blame us if we go up to that little kike and say, 'How you doing, old Marty Jewbaum?' 'Cause we'll be so glad to see him, we'll forget, that's all. No harm intended."

"No harm intended," laughed the red-haired one. "Yeah, if I was you two, I'd change my name too. Smith and Jones, that's what I'd call myselfs if I was you."

His friend cracked up.

The redhead looked Harry straight in the eye. "What'd you do, Greek? To be going under a fake name now?"

"Just policy, that's all," said Harry.

"Yeah, well, we got policy too," said the other. "And it don't include taking care of anybody but us. So stay out of our way, and won't nobody bother nobody, got it?"

"Got it," said Harry softly. He said to the two men, "Why are you here? Why *this* operation?"

"We are fighting the destruction of our race," said the blond one. "Him and me. Our race, that is. Course that don't include Jews and Greeks. It includes Americans. States are soft. Communists and Jews and faggots and niggers, that's what you got wherever you go. Faggots and niggers and Jews and communists. Got to start fighting it in the field, that's all."

"Case you haven't heard," said Harry, "the point of this operation is to put a black man back on the throne of Bashi."

"We *always* fight on the right side," said Mason. Or Dozier.

"We got these friends in Pretoria," said the other. "They let us know. They said this thing was okay. They were the ones put us up to it. We're gonna be fucking field marshals. We're gonna be able to mash us some nigger heads once we get in there. That's what we're doing it for. Pretoria promised."

The sadness in Harry's eyes was suddenly less than before. "Fine, guys," he said, stood up, and walked away.

Loudly, one of them said, "Hey, listen, why hasn't there ever been a Greek pope?"

"Why?" said the other.

"Well, there was one one time. But he died of old age before they ever figured out where It'ly was."

Rosie had been right, Harry knew. It was obvious what to do about Mason and Dozier.

That night Rosie was on guard. He stood at mock attention at the entranceway to the Prince's quarters. Marty was across the way in the small tent allotted to the guards. Harry was hidden in the shadows. It got very dark in the desert at night.

All three waited patiently. It might happen, it might not happen. What had been clear from Harry's conversation with Mason and Dozier—and from what Harry and Marty already knew of them—was that the two men would make trouble for the Black Berets if they possibly could. They had before, in 'Nam. Ten years difference, the fact that they were all ostensibly on the same side, wouldn't matter.

They waited, not knowing for sure whether Mason and Dozier would walk by the Prince's quarters that evening. Good chance of it though. Om-batu's plywood palace was set at the center of everything. It was the sole tourist attraction in the camp. All the new recruits walked by it, at least once, possibly hoping for a glance at the man who was giving them gold in exchange for putting their lives in danger.

Mason and Dozier did come by. They didn't know Rosie anyway, but he was wearing a hat pulled down low over his brow, just in case. All the rednecks could see that he was another nigger. The red-haired one spat as he walked by—it was a habit of his whenever he saw a coon trying to take a white man's place in the world. Coons had their own place, of course. At the bottom. The blond one just scowled. But before they had gotten well past Rosie, someone began to whistle a melancholy tune in the shadows. A slow, lilting tune that sounded ancient and mournful.

It was an old Greek song, sung by mothers to the children whose fathers are gone away—to sea, to war, to a place where they'll look on their children no more.

It was Harry's song, and Rosie and Marty knew it of old.

It was also a signal.

"*Assassins!*" Applebaum screamed. Nobody screamed like Marty—maybe a banshee did, maybe a man tortured to his last extremity, maybe a soul on the threshold of hell—but nobody else. "*Assassins!*"

Rosie shot his M-16 into the air, filling the airless desert night with echoing gunfire. Marty was still yelling.

Mason and Dozier were immediately on alert—but for what?

Not for Harry, anyway.

They didn't see him or the knife in his hands. And that's why the blond one—Mason, or was it Dozier?—didn't know what the burning sensation in his left side was. And he didn't understand how a point of pain could suddenly start to move in a line from his side, through his stomach, down into his belly. And that sudden, liquid warmth? And why did he suddenly feel like he

142

had lost weight—ten, twenty pounds? That was the only part he figured out, because by the sporadic firelight of Rosie's rifle, he saw his own guts spilled out on the ground in front of him. And then, as if he were making an attempt to gather them up again, or protect them from hungry dogs, he fell forward on top of them. He never figured out anything else again. It didn't matter to anybody anymore, not even to him, which one he had been—Mason or Dozier.

The other one, the red-haired one, he had a rifle. He got to see what was coming. Not at first though. At first something came at him from behind and knocked the rifle out of his hands with a quick, hard movement. It was strong and powerful and fast and left his hands stinging from the forced separation from his weapon. He spun around and there was—Applebaum. The name came quickly enough now, and he got it right.

"Hey, Marty—"

Marty Applebaum grinned, and kicked him in the stomach. He doubled right over, fell on the ground, turned over on his back, and began kicking. But not hard enough, not fast enough, not in the right direction. Because the Greek was coming in from the side, and the Greek had a knife, and out of the corner of his eye, he saw the sharp edge of the knife coming for his throat. Then the knife was in his throat. He had one last sensation of the cold metal, inside him—funny, at the last moment of your life, to experience something that was totally new. Then he was dead, of course, and it didn't matter to him who had done it.

"Don't like killing Americans," Applebaum said with quiet distaste.

"Don't let it bother you with these two," said Harry.

Marty looked up at his friend and seemed surprised. Hell, Harry didn't look any sadder this time. Harry usually got this real sad expression on his face every time he had to kill somebody. But for once it looked as if Harry hadn't regretted the necessity.

Suddenly, they were surrounded—by other guards, by mercenaries streaming out of their tents, by Prince Om-batu himself, wearing nothing but a pair of boxer shorts. Everybody was shouting, everybody was stumbling over the corpses of Mason and Dozier—they'd be buried in the same grave, which might have been a comfort to the two men, if they'd been told about it beforehand—everybody was demanding explanations in half a dozen languages.

But Marty was just looking at the Greek, that's all. And he said to himself, in a moment of quiet lucidity, *Somebody crazy as I am* . . .

22

Cowboy and Beeker had taken an Air France jet to Bashi-Bruges. Cowboy had dearly wanted a scotch when the Parisian stewardess offered them cocktails, but that one look from Beeker was more than enough to dissuade him. He wouldn't have minded having the stewardess as a consolation prize, but the memory of his last encounter aboard a plane put that out of his mind as well.

The landing was swift and easy. Almost good enough for even Cowboy to approve of the pilot's skill, though there was a little bump that Cowboy thought the Frenchman might have done without.

He and Beeker were dressed in tropical-weight suits. They had on plain sports shirts. Cowboy's boots were the only distinctive item of apparel on either of them. But as he walked behind Beeker through the muggy African heat, Cowboy was once again struck by how little difference clothes made on Beeker. You couldn't hide those muscles and you couldn't round off the corners of that military style. The square shoulders never softened and the meticulous pace never faltered. The man was a Marine through and through.

They got a cab—a tiny black thing without a meter and three tiny-statured black men in the front seat, none of whom spoke English. There didn't seem to be any street signs in Bashi-Bruges either, so it was a wonder that they got to their destination. Beeker registered. Cowboy carried the bags. Quicker than they had imagined it possible, they found themselves in their room on the sixth floor of the Bashi-Bruges Hilton. It was amazing. They had just been in Madrid, one of the most sophisticated capitals of Europe. Now they were here in one of the most primitive cities of Africa. The goddamn rooms were identical.

Whatever likeness in national characteristics the world might attempt to achieve through cultural exchanges, education, travel, and all the rest of it, Cowboy was certain that Hilton Hotels International was the only force that had a prayer of achieving it. The fucking place even had the same brand of soap here as in Spain and—Cowboy realized—probably the same as he could have found in the Shreveport Hilton.

Cowboy looked out the window over the city. There weren't more than half a dozen buildings in this city of a million and a half that were even as tall as the six-story Hilton. Cowboy could see a kind of compound of the very white and bright buildings that spelled government anywhere on the globe. One or two streets in the distance of what looked like big houses, surrounded by gardens with large mature trees—embassies and the five rich men Bashi could boast. Everything else was a hopeless, colorless maze of poverty and wretchedness, and it started right down below, twenty or thirty feet from the entrance to the hotel, but behind a stone wall so the guests wouldn't be upset when they first arrived from the airport.

"Place didn't seem jumpy," Cowboy said to Beeker. "Everybody friendly, nice as can be. No hassle with customs. No military that I could see. No guns. No dead bodies flying through the air from the latest truck-bomb attack. Nothing like that. You notice anything?"

"Place doesn't know enough to be jumpy," said Beeker. "You heard what Jacobson said. Bashi isn't on the Russian side, not on the American side either. Who's gonna give them intelligence? The French maybe, except this place was Belgian. Belgians aren't exactly known for their intelligence services. Nazis wiped 'em all out. Country never built up its military again. Besides, who're they gonna tell? Jamad? Nobody likes him 'cause he won't take sides. The military? The military are gonna be in on it. Announce it in the newspaper? Nobody can read. Parkes sure did pick the right place for a man of his talents."

Cowboy took off his jacket and saw the sweat marks showing everywhere the thin cotton shirt had touched his body. Place was as bad as 'Nam. The heat, the humidity. Only thing different was

146

the wind blew from a different direction, that's all. "So what's next? What we gonna do about this?"

Beeker was staring out the window, maybe seeing if he could sniff Parkes out. Maybe Parkes smelled that bad, that you could tell his stink even over the open sewers that ran alongside all the principal avenues of Bashi-Bruges.

"Billy Leaps, we are only two men. What are we gonna do?"

"Walk around," Beeker said softly. "Walk around and make sure somebody sees us."

"Tried that in Mexico City. Don't work," grumbled Cowboy.

It was evening by the time they left the hotel. Bashi-Bruges was too far from the coast to benefit from any cooling effects of the ocean. The hot, damp air came in every March, and sat around rotting until the following February. That's what it felt like in Bashi-Bruges.

Beeker carried a map, but for the first stop they climbed into another taxi. This time there were four tiny black men in the front seat, but still none of them spoke any English. But they got Cowboy and Beeker to the American Embassy all right.

They got out down the street, in front of a wall overgrown with vines and creepers. "Stay here," Beeker said. It was an order by a commander in the field. Cowboy didn't argue. He tried to be nonchalant as he leaned against the crumbling wall. So often Cowboy followed Beeker's orders without having any idea what the Cherokee was up to. This time he knew right off.

Of course. Cowboy sighed. How could he forget? Every American Embassy in the world has a detachment of *them* as guards. *Them* with their dress blues all starched and polished no matter what the heat. *Them* with their high inside haircuts and clean-shaven faces and scraping idolatry for ritual and discipline. Times Cowboy'd swear he was never going to escape from the goddamn United States Marine Corps.

And here was proof. Billy Leaps Beeker, with that ramrod-stiff demeanor telegraphing his membership in the Corps to his fellow fraternity member. Quick exchanges of information and emotion through clenched teeth. A whole goddamn international network of secretive brothers. *Fucking Marines.*

Beeker was done in a couple of minutes. He returned to where Cowboy waited for him. He didn't speak, just nodded his head for Cowboy to fall in and move along with him. Cowboy knew the gesture. He shook his head and kept on following Beeker through the Bashi-Bruges street.

The embassy district ended abruptly. One more crumbling vine-covered wall, then around the corner, slums. The worst that Cowboy had ever seen. Or smelled. If Applebaum had been there, he could have flattened ten thousand homes with a single Geronimo yell. Cardboard and tin and sewage—that was the impression you got. Everyone was starving, everyone was ill, everything stank. The people were too listless, too wracked with hunger and pain to do much protesting. They wandered around among the ramshackle dwellings as if they were looking for an unoccupied spot on which to lie down and die. Parkes, the ultimate bureaucrat, was fit king for a nation whose population lived in such unrelieved misery, poverty, disease, and distress.

Billy Leaps Beeker was a Cherokee. His sense of direction worked even here. He looked at the map, looked up at the sky, put the map in his pocket, and was off. Cowboy followed, breathing through his mouth so he wouldn't choke on the stench. Human stench was always so much worse than any other kind. Human shit, human corpses, human illness—they always smelled worse than any other kind.

They ended up in a bar, in a cellar of a house that looked like it had been shut up and abandoned by people who had moved to the slums in order to come up in the world. Cowboy didn't have to wonder why they were here. There were those haircuts. Those starched pants. Those clean-shaven faces. It was the hangout for the Embassy Marine detachment. Whole thing disgusted Cowboy. He watched Beeker exchange knowing glances with the others.

Cowboy got defensive when he was in the minority like this. It almost seemed like Beeker changed allegiances when he got in with Marines. Cowboy sent out private unspoken messages to these guys in the dark, damp cellar bar. Hey, that's okay. You think he's one of you guys. Maybe part of him is. But more of him's part of *us*. He may have started out as a Marine. He may still look like a Marine. But things happened to him in 'Nam that you guys can't even begin to imagine. But I can imagine them. 'Cause I was there. And those are the things that made him a Black Beret, and now he's *our* leader. So look but don't touch.

Mineral water. Fucking mineral water again. Bar was a goddamn sink hole in a city that was a cesspool in a country that was a swamp—and he had to drink goddamn mineral water.

He sat and fumed. But even though nobody talked to them, Cowboy'd already figured out what was happening. They were waiting.

Cowboy figured they'd have to wait for less than ten minutes. Marines were that goddamn punctual.

Eight minutes. That was when Cowboy saw a man—unmistakably one of *them*—standing in the doorway of the bar. Had a sack with him, like he was carrying a few six-packs. Except you didn't bring your six-packs to a bar.

He came over. Didn't shake hands. Didn't introduce himself. Put the bag on the table, and sat down.

The waitress came over. Beautiful black woman with a singsong voice. Cowboy knew the type. She'd fuck for a dollar, but by God she was gonna choose the wallet that dollar came out of. If she didn't want you, you couldn't have her for any price. She looked at the newcomer with eyes that said, *Fifty cents. A quarter.*

She didn't even notice Cowboy.

"Bottle of beer," the new man said.

She rushed to get it, and when she got back he took it from her. His hand grazed hers. She looked like she was going to faint with the thrill of it.

He waved her away. Eve must have had a look like that on her face when God threw her out of Eden.

"This is dangerous," the man finally said. He spoke to Beeker of course, ignored Cowboy. "Against every ordinance in the book. We could get in serious shit for this."

"You won't," said Beeker.

"Inventory's coming up. Looks real bad to have missing shit."

"You'll get 'em back," said Beeker. It was a statement of fact, not just a promise.

The newcomer wasn't up for a jovial talk. Now a pilot in the Air Corps, well they would have had a good time, Cowboy thought. Downed a few beers, talked about all kinds of shit, ended up drunk and propositioning that waitress together. This guy? Nah. He was just making a drop—Marine to Marine. He never even took a swig of the beer. Stood up. Nodded at Beeker like they were exchanging a secret handshake and walked out. That was it. Cowboy expected the waitress to commit suicide at the end of the bar.

Maybe she did, but Cowboy never found out. Beeker left money on the table—they took dollars here—and stood up. Cowboy followed him out.

Just before they emerged into the light, the Cherokee opened the bag and brought out two Colt .45s complete with shoulder holsters. Wherever there was a Marine, Beeker could get them armed. No need to fool with customs in a foreign country, so long as it had an American Embassy with a Marine guard attached.

They checked out the weapons. Everything was in order. Of course it was! Goddamn Marine weapons are always in order. They strapped on their shoulder holsters, pocketed the extra clips, and stepped out into the startling African twilight. The sky was shining dark blue, and it seemed to steep everything around them in the same deep blue tones. It was an uncomfortable sensation, as if a new blue sun had appeared in the old familiar sky, and sunlight forever after was going to be very different.

They were near the equator, however, and twilight didn't last long. By the time they got to the next bar, it was night. Black night, and the neon in Bashi-Bruges was as garish as neon was in Amsterdam, in Djakarta, in Vegas. And the women were as available, and almost as expensive. The currency change, that was all.

But Cowboy wasn't allowed to sample the women, though he wouldn't have minded the opportunity to increase his fund of knowledge about African ladies. Probably they were as nice, in their way, as Spanish ladies. And he'd never been married in Africa. Nowhere on the whole goddamn continent. He wondered what a native Bashi wedding was like. Probably the bride had to wear the skull of her dead father around her neck on the wedding night, something like that. Cowboy could take it.

What he couldn't take was the mineral water. Made you piss worse than beer. Sat in the pit of your stomach worse than hard cheese. Tightened your sinews worse than sour berries. He was going to die if he didn't get a scotch.

But they were in the field. That meant no scotch, no women. Cowboy began dreaming of making a return trip to Vegas. And not with the Berets. Maybe just take Tsali. The kid wouldn't look at him funny if he wanted a second drink, or if he eyed the women, or even if he scored a gram at the dark end of the hotel corridor.

Bashi-Bruges might have had its pleasures—what capital city didn't?—but Cowboy never got to taste any of them. Beeker just kept leading the way from one bar to another through the dark streets, following the crosses marked on the map in his pocket. One bar was like another, except that usually it was tawdrier and lower than the last. They all had vaguely French names, they all had the same five hookers occupying the last five stools at the end of the same leather-padded bar, the same songs on the jukebox, the same scars on the top of the little rickety tables, the same boozy foreign businessmen, the same skinny Arab pickpocket. Maybe Beeker was just leading him in a circle. If so, they had begun to repeat a long time ago.

Then they came to a place that was different. Cowboy could feel the change, even though the name—Le Bistro—was the same, and the decor was the same, and the same goddamn five hookers sat on the same goddamn five stools at the end of the bar. It was the clientele. He hadn't seen these men before. He would have remembered. They were as unmistakable as the Marines had been. They were military in their own fashion, even out of uniform. They were all natives. But they were the only men Beeker and Cowboy had seen the whole day who seemed to be on alert. All the nervousness Cowboy had expected to find on the streets when they arrived earlier in the day was concentrated in this tiny bar, up one flight of stairs from a nameless dark street. The suspicion, the anxiety, the tight-fisted drinking—all of it was thick in the stale smoky air.

Cowboy suddenly wasn't thinking of scotch and women. The shoulder holster was no longer an intrusive piece of Marine Corps hardware. It had just become his best friend. He was blood brother to that .45. And he was very pleased to have made the acquaintance of the man who brought it to Billy Leaps in a paper sack.

Cowboy and Beeker didn't have to exchange a word. They scanned the crowd in what must have seemed an offhand, oblivious manner, as if looking for a friend they already knew was on another continent.

"What do you think?" asked Beeker, as he took a bottle of mineral water from the bartender. He held it, raised it to his lips, didn't drink even that sip.

"Feels like the night before," Cowboy said, remembering the way American troops had acted the night before they went into the Vietnam jungle. Some strange combination of anticipation, exaltation, and fear was mixed in the men at those moments. The knowledge that they were about to go into battle—the very thing that they had been trained for—and the very real fear of dying, of ceasing to exist, always produced this strange alchemy. It was something you could smell sometimes. You could read it in the eyes. It was certainly unmistakable to the sense of a man who'd experienced it as often as Cowboy.

"I figure," said Beeker, "that by the way we've gone around town and dropped money, and made ourselves conspicuous, Parkes must know we're here. And if he doesn't yet, somebody in this bar is sure gonna take the opportunity to tell him."

Beeker was probably right, Cowboy decided. There'd be action soon. For something as big and as important as what Parkes had planned, he couldn't take the chance of even just two un-uniformed military men wandering about this way. You can't let unknown factors like that go unrestrained at so crucial a time. And Parkes had a whole country at stake.

A group of four natives came into the bar. They took the only free table, diagonally across the room from where Beeker and Cowboy sat. They had that same military demeanor: soliders, no doubt about it. But they weren't just experiencing the Night Before. They were looking for something that was easy to spot in Bashi-Bruges: two white men sipping mineral water in a bar where they weren't known.

"Here?" Cowboy asked in a low voice.

Beeker looked around casually. Fifty men, thereabouts, in the bar. Only a handful of Caucasians. Only a few others not identifiably members of the Bashi military. "No," he decided.

Cowboy nodded, downed his mineral water as if it were Black Label, and stood up from the table. Beeker joined him and they walked out the door, knowing full well they'd have company in about five seconds.

A warrior on peak works automatically. He senses the terrain more than he studies it. It took Beeker and Cowboy no more than a count of ten to position themselves in the shadows to the right of the bar's entrance. Downtown and their hotel were off to the left. The four men following them would assume they had gone that way.

Cowboy and Beeker had their Colts out, hammers back and safeties off. The four men appeared quickly. Too quickly. They weren't the most formidable opponents. But that didn't mean that Cowboy and Beeker ceased to regard them as enemies to be taken out with all possible care and finesse.

The four Bashi men seemed surprised not to see their quarry. They spoke hurriedly, and none too quietly. They walked too quickly toward the downtown section. A block away, with the Black Berets hidden in another set of shadows behind them, they conferred briefly, and split up, two and two.

Beeker made only a tiny motion with his hand. Cowboy understood it. They followed the pair that went off in the left-hand direction, down a darker street. Cowboy and Beeker followed, soundlessly. That wasn't hard when the street was filled with rotting garbage. It made for soft, silent progress.

The two Bashi were talking to one another, peering into the darkness ahead. They never bothered to glance behind them, and neither of them heard Beeker's silent approach until he took out the right-hand man with a crushing choke hold. Cowboy grabbed the other and dragged him into an alleyway that was not much more than a depression in the crumbling row of buildings along that unlighted street.

Faint music, a wailing love song in the Bashi language, wafted from a window somewhere above. A man and woman, obviously drunk, staggered along the street. They lurched over the man who lay facedown in the garbage, but otherwise took no notice of him. Their laughter faded gradually away.

"Parkes" was the one word Cowboy said. He had his hand over the Bashi soldier's mouth, and the man's arm twisted painfully upward behind him. The oldest hold in the book, but nonetheless effective for its antiquity. Pain was pain.

153

The man shook his head.

He was going to play hero.

"None of this shit," said Beeker. "I'm tired."

"Okay," said Cowboy. "Parkes," he said once more.

The Bashi shook his head.

Cowboy made one sudden movement, and there was a crack. Simultaneous with that splintering bone, Beeker reached out and shoved the man's jaw upward, smashing teeth and stifling the scream. The Bashi soldier gagged, and when he was able to open his mouth, a little piece of bleeding flesh fell out. He'd bitten off the end of his tongue.

"The arm was one," said Beeker. "The jaw was two. Here comes three."

He put a knee in the man's groin. Sounds simple, but to the Bashi soldier it felt like all the tortures of eternal hell had been squeezed into one single place on his body. He fell, writhing on the ground.

"Parkes," said Cowboy for the third time.

The man continued to writhe, but it was obvious that he was trying to speak.

"Da-goman," he gasped at last, and pointed off toward the left. He didn't speak English, but he held up three trembling fingers. "Da-goman. Da-goman."

"General Da-goman," said Beeker.

"Three blocks?" Cowboy said.

The man didn't understand. He kept flashing three fingers at them, insistently, and speaking words that neither Cowboy nor Beeker understood.

"Take us there," said Cowboy, suddenly pulling the man up onto his wobbling legs.

The man evidently understood Cowboy. He certainly understood what would happen if he didn't comply. He did his best to stagger forward. Beeker helped him.

"So Parkes is at General Da-goman's. Shouldn't we have figured that out? From what Jacobson told us this morning?"

"I knew where Parkes was," said Beeker, over the Bashi soldier's stooping shoulder. "I just wanted him to know we were coming."

23

If there had ever been any doubt in the Prince's feelings about his new bodyguards, the incident with the two redneck intruders solved that. It became noised about the camp that the two dead men had been violently racist, so no wonder that they had made an attempt on Om-batu's life.

It had been an easy setup for the Black Berets: to get rid of two men who would have delighted in creating havoc with their larger plans, and at the same time convince both the Prince and Major Ascham that their services were required absolutely.

They had become something of heroes in the camp. That was good and that was bad. It was good in that it allowed them free reign to poke about wherever they pleased. This was especially helpful to Applebaum, who found out everything there was to know about the airstrip and the arsenal. It was bad in that it cast them in a whole series of very peculiar roles. They had to listen to the communists talk about their role in the furtherance of the cause of world revolution. The Palestinians were certain that the Black Berets were going to help them in their work against the Tel-Aviv/Washington axis. And so on, through a dozen conflicting fanatical causes. It was hard to keep Applebaum quiet when they were approached like that, but Rosie said shut up, and Rosie was Marty's field commander. It hurt, but Marty said nothing.

The day arrived. December 20. The invasion. The Prince would be replaced on the throne of his father.

Even if Rosie hadn't been allowed inside the Prince's quarters at all hours, he would have known what was coming. You could sense it in the air of the camp. You didn't always have to tell lower-echelon troops when they were being sent out. They could sense it, the way the Chinese say that cattle and fowl can feel when an earthquake is coming on.

The plan was simple. Rosie heard it from Major Asshole's own lips. With some troops already in Bashi-Bruges, the invading forces had only two goals. First, to secure the airport, the only strip in Bashi that could accommodate planes that might fly in numbers of opposing troops. Second, they would lead the attack on the barracks and the presidential palace.

The mercenary army was filed along the airstrip for a final inspection. Mercenary was a kind word, however. A mercenary was a man—or a woman—who fought for a cause not his own, in proper exchange for money. There was honor in that, Rosie thought. To sell the possibility of one's own death, there was nothing wrong there. It was certainly better than rubbing away the minutes, hours, days, and years of your life behind a scarred desk in a windowless office in a dusty town in a state ruled by corruption. In the end, you died all the same. There was no escaping the end, was there? Not for anybody.

The plan was for the forces to fly from this base to Bashi-Bruges. Take the airport, secure it. Then the last plane, the one carrying the Prince, Major Ascham, and the Prince's honor guard, would arrive. That had been the frosting on Rosie's cake, for all three Black Berets to be assigned to this last flight. It wasn't even scheduled to leave for an hour after the others.

Relishing their parts, Harry, Rosie, and Marty saluted the mercs as they embarked. The Prince was pleased with the pomp and circumstance. He announced that Field Marshal Abdul Muhamed's first responsibility, upon the restoration of the throne of Om-batu's father, was to organize a band to play on such ceremonial occasions as this.

Rosie bowed his head in submission, and at the same time kicked at Applebaum. Damn little psychopath could blow everything with his jumpy anxiousness, his incessant toothy grinning.

Applebaum quieted, a little.

The engines of the Fokkers revved up. The planes, now fully loaded, began to taxi to the end of the makeshift runway. As though they were trying to put on a show for the few spectators left on the ground, the pilots placed their machines dangerously close together. Only a man like Cowboy should pull that kind of stunt. And these pilots weren't Cowboy.

With an even louder noise, first one, then the rest of the planes took off up the runway. Rosie stared, admiring the beauty of flight. Once the landing gear was up, the sleek lines of the planes became much more apparent. He watched them climb high, higher, higher . . .

"Now!" Marty screamed. *"Now!"*

As though Applebaum's voice had activated the bomb, the first of the Fokkers exploded into an orange and black sunburst of dazzling intensity.

The other three planes immediately veered away, the two on either side turning left and right, the fourth, directly behind the explosion, climbing suddenly higher.

Then, of course, there were three more explosions, three more orange and black sunbursts, that occurred more or less simultaneously.

Applebaum grinned. He had planned it to happen that way. Like they were goddamn fireworks.

Goddamn beautiful fireworks, though. Just fucking beautiful.

The low baritone explosions reached them just a moment later. *BOOOM.* Then *BOO/BOO/BOOOOM.*

The planes were already a couple of miles away, but the whole sky in that direction was littered with burning debris and black oily smoke. Rosie even saw a parachute open, and thought, *Great Christ, somebody survived that hell*—but then the parachute burst into yellow flame as well.

Prince Om-batu and Ascham were staring stuporous and open-mouthed. Behind them stood the two pilots who were to fly the fifth Fokker to Bashi-Bruges.

Much farther back were the camp personnel—about fifteen people—who had come out to watch the departure. Marty turned around and showed them his M-60. They all fled back into the camp, like cockroaches when the kitchen light is turned on.

Harry took the two pilots. "Down, fast, face flat or you don't have a face left." His M-16 was aimed at their heads, and they weren't about to argue or ask questions. The aerial display was still a mystery. No mystery, though, about the barrel of an M-16 when you can see the light reflecting off the inside of the barrel. They fell, fast and hard, onto the asphalt.

The Major at least had a moment when he tried to act like a soldier. Rosie hadn't expected that, and he was glad. Even an asshole had the right to make his exit good. The Major reached for the pistol that rested in a holster at his waist. He dragged it out. But not quite fast enough.

Rosie backed away a couple of steps. It was hard to take careful aim with an M-16, at so close a target.

First the Major's hand.

It seemed to disintegrate, and the warped pistol fell to the airstrip pavement.

The Major looked at Rosie disbelieving.

Is he seeing me? Rosie wondered. *Or his own death?*

But who knew what the dying thought? They didn't come back to tell. And Major Asshole was dead, with another bullet in his throat, and a third right through his heart.

Rosie had thought many times that he'd take pleasure in killing this man. *But when the time had come, it had just been . . . Pop. Pop. Pop. You're dead. And that's that.*

"Wasn't that great!" Applebaum was screaming, jumping up and down on the pavement, and all but tossing the M-60 into the air in his glee.

The pilots were still frozen in position. They weren't about to look at what was going on. They just prayed that nobody's weapon went off accidentally.

Prince Om-batu, heir presumptive to the throne of the sovereign state of Bashi, had puked. The remains of a large lamb dinner were now splattered all over the corpse of Major Ronald Ascham.

The obese black man finished up with a series of coughs and dry heavings. "Who are you?" he wheezed. "Did you do this?" he said, pointing vaguely into the sky, which looked oily with the smoke of the debris of the four downed Fokkers. "Why did—"

"I didn't," said Rosie. "Marty here took care of that. Little bomb on each of those planes set to go off when the planes got to a certain altitude."

"That was a piece of work!" protested Applebaum. "You hear that rhythm? *Boom. Boo/Boo/Boooom.* That's not easy.

158

That's hard. To get that kind of rhythm going. Especially if you got to depend on pilots that don't know what they're doing."

Om-batu was still in a daze, but he wasn't so confused that he forgot he was still in danger. He hadn't been killed yet, but these three men—who knew what they'd do?

"I'll give you gold, all my gold," he offered Rosie.

"Nice," said Rosie. "Let's you and me go get that gold. My friends here still got a little work to do."

There wasn't any hurry now, of course, because it didn't matter when that last Fokker got to Bashi-Bruges. Because the other four weren't going to make it there at all.

Harry and Marty took the pilots onto the plane, and tied them up there, then they returned to the camp. Applebaum emptied all the explosives left by the troops into a truck and began setting up explosives at key points. He would have liked to do the job just right, but there just wasn't time. Cowboy and Beeker were probably already in Bashi-Bruges, wondering what was keeping them. So Marty was working quickly.

Over the camp's loudspeaker system, Harry announced, "Whoever's left in the camp go to the old ruined village. Take your personal belongings, some food, and a tent with you. This camp will be leveled within the hour. You won't be harmed or hurt, but only if you take refuge in the camp. Anyone found with arms will be shot."

He didn't repeat the message. He didn't need to. The Italian medical team, the cooks and truck drivers, gathered up hurriedly and huddled together at the far side of the ruined Libyan village, as far away from the camp as possible. Harry visited them once, and was surprised to find them neither frightened, nor angry, nor sullen, nor even particularly disturbed. These were the true mercenaries of this operation, he thought, the ones who took whatever comes.

"We'll send someone for you," he said. "But it may be in a day or two."

In the Prince's quarters, the Prince threw aside the wall hangings and carpets that were piled at the back, and drew out three large attaché cases.

"What about the safe?" Rosie asked.

"Everything has been taken out of the safe," replied Om-batu nervously. "Major Ascham and I were taking all this with us today. It is ready to go." He opened one of the cases. It was neatly packed to the top with small bars of gold. Still holding the M-16 pointed at the Prince, Rosie reached in and took out one of the bars. One hundred grams, with the mark of a Zurich bank.

"This is Bashi gold," said Rosie. "You stole it from your people."

"No, no," said Om-batu. "When I came out I had nothing. My father was stripped of everything. My brothers had gold. And diamonds too, but when they died, everything was lost. I had nothing. Nothing."

"Then where did this gold come from?"

"Major Ascham."

"And he got it from Parkes."

"Yes, I think so. I think it is Parkes's gold. We were taking it to Parkes today."

So, Parkes had been richer than they had imagined. Very rich, if he could afford to leave this much gold in a Libyan training camp. Rosie did some quick figuring. He had been offered $7,500 up front for this stint and $7,500 on arrival in the capital. He figured that was high, and that the average mercenary hadn't been promised more than $10,000. At three hundred mercenaries, plus some support personnel, plus money for supplies—Libyans didn't trust their own currency, and for political reasons wouldn't trade in dollars—there must be nearly two million dollars worth of gold.

Not bad for a few weeks' work in the desert.

"Fine," said Rosie. "Real fine. You bring 'em out to the plane."

The cases were heavy, but the Prince didn't complain. Maybe it was in his blood. His grandfather had been a bearer back in the twenties, and had gotten whipped to death by his Belgian employer for dropping a box of scientific instruments, none of which, it turned out, had been damaged.

"All right," said Rosie resignedly from the door of the plane. "Let's see it."

"No, no," said Applebaum, "don't watch. You don't have to

watch. I didn't have time to do any real interesting shit. It's just gonna go, that's all."

"Then let's see it go."

Applebaum grimaced, then ran back to the little shack on the edge of the strip. He went inside for a few moments, then ran back out. Waving his arms frantically, he motioned them all into the plane. "All right," he screamed, "let's get this fucker off the ground."

They saw the explosions from the air. Applebaum was glum, and wouldn't even look out the window. "I hate rush jobs," he complained. "I hate 'em, I hate 'em, I hate 'em. I'm just glad Beeker's not here. Beeker would kill me."

That was all in Applebaum's mind, of course.

He managed the job just fine. He was probably the only man on the African continent who might have watched and decided that the job lacked finesse.

There were seven separate explosions, and it was apparent, even before the smoke had cleared, that nothing at all was going to be left of Parkes's Libyan camp.

The pilot, with a gun to his neck, turned the plane and headed for Bashi-Bruges.

24

The wounded Bashi soldier led them to General Da-goman's home. It was directly at the rear of the presidential palace, even sharing a common garden wall. When Parkes took over, he wasn't going to have to go very far. That was the kind of joke that a man like Parkes enjoyed.

There were two guards. The doorway was double, but there were no windows on the street. More than two guards might well have drawn more attention to the house than Parkes and General Da-goman relished.

The broken-armed Bashi soldier served one more purpose. In the darkness, he looked like a drunken man being supported by two friends. When they got within such distance of the guards that Cowboy and Beeker were in danger of being recognized as white men, even on that unlighted avenue, Beeker pushed the man forward. He staggered forward and fell right at the feet of the guards, unconscious.

That was all Beeker and Cowboy needed. They were right on top of the guards then. Cowboy was a simple fighter—fast, vicious, direct. He kicked his man in the groin . . . hard. When the man doubled over, Cowboy kindly helped him on down to the ground and smashed his head on the concrete. Billy Leaps was simply overpowering. He hit the guard in the throat with a punch that carried all the anger he'd been carrying since this episode began. It wouldn't be necessary to tie either of these men.

The two Black Berets stepped through the carved wooden gate into the General's compound.

It's the foot soldier who suffers the night before, who worries about the next day's battle, who has to wonder if he'll see another sunset. The ones who send him to war and death don't necessarily share those anxieties. For the most part, generals are no more likely to die of violence than, say, bank presidents or actuaries. They spend the night before with bottles of Courvoisier VSOP and dream of another few ounces of enameled tin for their uniform jackets, of sudden promotion. They don't think particularly of the men who are almost sure to die, even if the battle is won.

And if the battle is lost? There's another battle down the line. But even if the regime topples, the whole country falls, there's always an exit planned for the leaders. A pilot waiting in an obscure corner of the airfield, a refuge in a friendly country, a bodyguard who also knows how to mix a good drink.

Parkes was like that, and so was General Da-goman. Cowboy and Beeker saw them through the narrow courtyard window that looked into the General's private apartments. Parkes they hadn't seen in twelve years, not since Saigon. He had grown bigger, of course, big right around the middle. Desk-sitting did it. Desk-sitting and too much Courvoisier VSOP. The bottle was turned so they could see the goddamned label. Da-goman they recognized from one of the photographs in the packet that Delilah had delivered to Cowboy in Madrid. Beeker didn't know who Delilah worked for, but by God, her information was of more use than the CIA's.

There was a third man, white, but neither Cowboy nor Beeker recognized him.

Beeker paused a few moments. Cowboy punched him once, a signal urging him on. They didn't know how long before they were discovered by other guards, before someone found the corpses in the doorway and raised an alarm.

Beeker still waited. He was savoring this moment.

Then that momentary pleasure turned sour in Beeker's mouth. Revenge wasn't his style, he realized. Revenge belonged to men like Parkes. It was always petty, no matter how it was carried out. This was not revenge, this was survival. That was all.

Parkes had betrayed them by sending them into Laos on a false, meretricious mission. He had manipulated them. He even tried to have them exterminated.

But ultimately, Billy Leaps couldn't be sorry all that had happened.

Because of Parkes the team was back together.

Because of the mission to Laos, they were all rich.

None of that would have happened without Parkes.

Still, Parkes would die for that.

Beeker stood a couple of feet back from the window, thickly paned with glass. He took note of the distance, saw that the two men on either side of Parkes wouldn't be able to move quickly enough.

The glass shattered inward as Beeker fired two shots, one toward the left, the other toward the right. Cowboy raced back toward the door, .45 held ready.

Two men were dead. The white man's chair tilted backward, and fell. His head cracked open on the floor—needlessly, because he was already dead.

General Da-goman, beefy as most African generals are, wavered in his chair a moment, then slipped over to the side awkwardly.

Parkes's brandy snifter was at his lips when the shots were fired. Without removing it, he glanced to the left and the right. He saw his two companions were dead, in the midst of their laughter at a joke Parkes had just told them. One small hole in the center of each forehead. General Da-goman's blood dribbled onto the floor. As the echo of the shots died away, the drip, drip, drip was the only sound he heard.

Parkes slowly put down the snifter.

He turned slowly in his chair, about to get up.

"Nope," said Cowboy, from the doorway of the room. The lights led him to the right place. A bodyguard in the kitchen would never finish his sandwich.

"Mr. Hatcher," stammered Parkes. "Is that you?"

"Sure is." Cowboy grinned. He waved the Colt toward the broken window. "And that's Mr. Beeker out there, Mr. Parkes. Mr. Beeker just shot your two friends. Well, here's Mr. Beeker now, Mr. Parkes."

"Mr. Hatcher—" began Parkes quickly. There was fear on his face. Palpable fear mixed with the perspiration that beaded on his forehead. Woodrow Wilson Parkes had always had his way. He could talk his way in one side of a hopeful situation and out the other when his own incompetence had turned it into a disaster.

With a few thousand carefully chosen words, he could make someone else's success his own, and with another thousand in the right ear, have someone else blamed for his own failures. He was beginning on that now. "Mr. Hatcher, you and Mr. Beeker have just committed a grave error. I'm saying this as your—"

Beeker very simply raised his arm. His gun fired once more.

Without warning, without explanation, without reproach.

One shot, right through the center of the forehead.

Parkes's mouth fell slack. Whatever word he intended to speak next was lodged forever in his throat.

Cowboy was disappointed. "Hey, Beak, I thought we were gonna have some fun with him. I had all this shit planned."

"Every second that man stayed alive was a second he was planning his escape. Keep us talking. Wait for more guards to show. He would have begged us to torture him because it kept him alive that much longer."

Cowboy understood. That casualness in Beeker's third shot was the ultimate insult for Woodrow Wilson Parkes. He died dishonored. Shot like a mad dog in the sun-struck street.

A stink rose up from his corpse. In the last fearful moments of his life, Woodrow Wilson Parkes's bowels had opened up. He died wallowing in a pile of his own shit.

Bashi was peaceful the next day. A few soldiers wandered about waiting for orders that never came, but even they quieted down when Colonel Jamad announced the tragic murder of General Da-goman and two of his associates by unknown intruders. The two .45s were returned to the Marines at the American Embassy plenty of time before inventory. No one was the wiser.

When Cowboy and Beeker had returned to the Bashi-Bruges Hilton half an hour after Parkes's death, they had found Harry, Marty, and Rosie waiting for them in the hotel bar—all three of them with bottles of mineral water before them.

So far as they knew, they were still on battle alert.

Beeker bought a single bottle of whiskey at the bar, and carried it upstairs. The others followed. Billy Leaps Beeker poured out one glass all around. "To us," he said. "The Black Berets, and the successful completion of our mission. Parkes is dead."

Rosie grinned. "His camp is dust."

Positively poetic, when he wanted to be.

"To us," said Beeker, "in the field."

"And to us at home," added Cowboy.

"Tsali," said Harry, raising his own glass a little higher.

"And hot death to anybody who opposes us," concluded Marty, still with the maniacal smile.

They drank.

Afterward, Rosie retold all events in the camp.

"Goddamn," Cowboy whistled. "Fokkers. Wish I could have been there."

"A good job," Beeker concluded, and if Rosie and Harry and Applebaum had come out of the mission with nothing more than this one indication of Beeker's approbation, the whole business would have been worth it.

After that, Beeker went into the next room and got on the telephone. He was in there more than an hour. Bashi's telephone service was about on a level with its sewage and street-lighting works. When he came back, he said, "That clears up some things for us."

"You talk to her?" asked Cowboy. Meaning Delilah.

"Yeah, I got her. Think I sort of interrupted something with somebody. She's gonna fix things up for us. Om-batu goes free. He's harmless without somebody like Parkes backing him. Got a wife and kids somewhere, and he'll wander back to them, she guesses."

"The gold?" Rosie wanted to know.

Beeker grinned. "It was Parkes's. She's sure of that. But she suggested—and I agree—it would be a nice gesture if we left President Jamad one of the cases. As a token of our esteem that will also ensure an easy exit for us."

Everybody agreed. Two cases of gold would be plenty for them—since they didn't need any of it anyway.

"She had a message for you, Marty."

"For me?" His surprise was genuine, and he actually blushed.

"Yeah. She said to tell you they knew the camp was gone because they picked up the explosions on a seismograph in Cairo."

"Oh God! I'm a fucking earthquake!" Applebaum shouted,

jumping up and down on the bed, and swinging both arms like windmills.

"Fact is," said Beeker, after Harry had calmed Applebaum down a little, "Delilah had a lot to say. She wanted to remind us what day this was."

Harry checked his watch. "Twentieth."

"Of December. Christmas is coming up. And Tsali shot a deer, so we'll be having venison."

"How does she know that?" Cowboy demanded.

"She's been in touch with the boy, on that fucking computer you gave him. Those two talk every day. And she said one other thing, too."

"Yeah?" said Rosie. "What else?"

Beeker paused only a moment. "That there was more work for the Black Berets. Any time they wanted it."

They learned their deadly skills on the secret battlefields of Southeast Asia. They were brought back together by a betrayer's secrets. Now, they're going into business for themselves in

BLACK PALM

Black Berets #3 by Mike McCray

I am forty years old. I am the Prime Minister of the Republic of New Neuzen. I am a well-educated woman, the chosen leader of my people. I am a respected member of the leadership of the Free World. Three days ago I addressed the General Assembly of the United Nations.

Beatrix VanderVolt kept on saying those words to herself. Over and over again. She had to remember them to keep from going crazy.

After all, here she was hiding in a concrete bunker in the middle of the Louisiana wilderness, with nothing between her and an assassin's bullet but a hirsute Greek giant named Harry and a bespectacled little madman who looked as if he'd answer to anything, but most often answered to Marty.

Beep . . . beep . . . beep . . .

Both men moved quickly to the back of the house, toward a door that Beatrix had never seen open. She followed and found their faces intently studying a set of amber computer screens.

One screen in particular held their attention. "There

gotta be at least twenty of 'em. Jesus Christ!'' Harry spoke with unusual vehemence.

"More." Marty's voice was the opposite—calm for once, concentrated. This reversal of their usual manners made Beatrix uneasy. It suggested that whatever bothered them was a serious affair.

"Obviously going frontal," said Harry. "No cute tricks on the side. No pincer movements. . . ." He was studying the screen aloud. "Won't be nice," he concluded.

"We can do it," Marty said, but without his usual bravado.

Both men continued to monitor the screen. Then Harry said, "You know where they're headed don't you?"

"Oh, Jesus," exclaimed the other man, with a grin. His little eyes bulged behind his spectacles. "Oh, Jesus, Harry, can we do it? Can we really?"

Harry raised himself erect and turned to the Prime Minister. "You nearly got it in Washington. If we don't stop this little group coming this way, you may get it in Louisiana instead. We're gonna try to stop 'em, but we need your help."

"Anything." Beatrix VanderVolt meant it. She had seen the look on her assailants' faces the last time, when Beeker had saved her. She had found out much about the Black Palm in the meantime. And though she hated violence, and loathed the thought that her protection might be the cause of the deaths of others, she had no intention of dying.

Harry led the Prime Minister back to the large living area. A moment later Marty appeared again, carrying a small portable console, about the size of a typewriter keyboard, but with two rows of switches instead of keys.

"The charges are set to go," he said quickly. "Hooked up to electronic detonators. When you get the signal, just flip the switches. Fast as you can, any order. But it'll be neater if you work from both sides in toward the middle. Got it?"

"What's the signal?" she asked.

"A yellow flare," said Harry.

"What we're gonna try to do," said Marty, "is push these guys in together, real close. Maybe back 'em up a little bit, and get 'em to go where we want 'em to be. So all you have to do—"

"Is sit out on the porch," Harry went on, taking up Marty's instructions seamlessly, "and when you see the flare, start flipping the switches."

How deceptively quiet it is.

At first Beatrix was sure she meant the night. But the night and the stars weren't what was so absurdly quiet. She had been thinking about the thing on her lap. The little metal board with two dozen switches on it.

The decision to use the machine frightened her. No, that wasn't quite it. What frightened her was the ease with which she had made the decision to put her own safety above the lives of the twenty men who had come to kill her. She scanned the sky, waiting for Harry's yellow signal.

The flares were brilliantly yellow as they carved their way into the sky, one from either side. Their paths crossed elegantly directly above her. *How beautiful, she thought.* But even then she was flipping the switches, from the outside in, just as Marty had told her.

And with the very first switch there was an answer.

BOOOOOM!

Then one after the other, overlapping as her fingers

had overlapped. She watched in awe. The whole sky before her was lighted up, orange and yellow, great arcs of colored destruction. And little black silhouettes—like clever paper cutouts against the orange and yellow—of tree trunks, and branches, and men's legs, and men's torsos, and men's arms still clutching their useless stick rifles.

And what was most appalling, the Prime Minister thought, was that the scene really did have a kind of structure and rhythm, like a good fireworks display. High blasts and low blasts. Orange blasts with a hint of red. Yellow blasts with a hint of blue. A blast on one side countered by a blast on the other, and a third blast in the middle overpowering them both.

An artist! Martin Applebaum, in his thick glasses, was an artist with explosions. *A Michelangelo of death. A Leonardo of destruction. An artist!*